Sonny and the Heroic Deeds

Withdrawn Stock
Dorset Libraries

JENNIFER HASHMI

authorHOUSE®

AuthorHouse™ UK
1663 Liberty Drive
Bloomington, IN 47403 USA
www.authorhouse.co.uk
Phone: 0800.197.4150

Published by AuthorHouse 04/21/2016

ISBN: 978-1-5246-3255-7 (sc)
ISBN: 978-1-5246-3254-0 (e)

Contents

Chapter One

Time Has Passed

Time had passed since Pym's unfortunate trip to Sonny's house, and Sonny and Gogo were about to celebrate their twelfth birthdays. Gogo's father, Murgo Pongo, planned a joint birthday party for them. Sonny's 11+ exams were behind him and he felt free to enjoy himself. Gogo's end-of-year exams also were completed, so he too was in the mood for some fun. Murgo planned to hold the party in the meadow at the bottom of their hill which the owls used as their landing and take-off ground. It was here also that the Annual Trade Fair was held when it was Pongoland's turn to be host. There was plenty of space to put up tables for food as well as a dais for a rock concert Murgo had organized. Murgo was the King of Pongoland's First Minister, so he knew all the families on the Island. Everyone was invited.

Pongoland was an Island in the sky, and one of many Islands which existed in a slightly different dimension from our own. Sonny was a human boy whom Gogo had met several years earlier on a trip he made into our world. He struck up a close friendship with Sonny, and started to take him back to Pongoland nearly every weekend. The only way for a human child to go to Pongoland was if he was taken there by one of Murgo's family. The people of the Islands were about two feet tall by human measurement, so in order to go there at all Sonny had to shrink. There was a mystic knowledge of the way things work in the Islands. It was never spoken of and Sonny never asked questions, but things could be caused to happen which would be considered impossible in our world. Gogo would simply take Sonny by the hand and he would become the same height as Gogo which was about a foot tall at the beginning. Now they were sixteen inches tall according to our world's measurement. Together they would climb on to the back of Murgo's owl, Goggles, and fly away over the tree-tops and under the stars.

The mode of transport on the Islands was birds. Each Island had its' own birds to carry people back and forth between the Islands, as well as inland sometimes. The populations of the Islands differed, as did the life-styles to some extent, but each Island was governed by a King. Each Island had its' own royal family, and usually, but not always, the princes and princesses inter-married amongst themselves. This practice had built up a very close relationship between the Islands.

Sonny had visited several of the Islands close to Pongoland, but he couldn't travel far as he had to be back in his bed before morning at home. When it was night-time in Pongoland it was day-time at home, so Sonny's trips had to take place between going to bed Friday night and sunrise Saturday morning. Gogo had been bought in a toyshop by Sonny's Uncle for Sonny's birthday. Gogo had merely been looking at the toys when he was mistaken for one himself, and bought! For self-defence he had had to keep completely still, and to this day Sonny's parents thought he was a toy. If he didn't return to Pongoland after bringing Sonny home he spent the day sleeping on his bed. Sonny had developed the habit of having a long afternoon sleep on Saturday so that he could return to Pongoland Saturday night.

By now Sonny was very well-known indeed in Pongoland because of the many adventures Sonny, Gogo, and his younger brother Tobo, had been involved in. The King liked Sonny because he had so often, in times of crisis, seen solutions which did not occur to Pongo people. Sonny's imagination worked differently, but Gogo was always an eager comrade in all their adventures, and over the years Gogo and Tobo had developed some of Sonny's capacity to trace a very simple logic running through an apparent conundrum. Gogo's parents treated Sonny like their own child, and so were very keen that he should celebrate his twelfth birthday with Gogo. That was besides the celebrations organized at home by his own parents. The twelfth birthday was a mile-stone in

2

the lives of Island children. They continued to go to school, but began also to learn a trade or craft.

In general, occupations were passed down in families from generation to generation. Thus the miners of the precious stones and minerals to be found in the Pongoland hills taught their sons to dig and to evaluate their finds. Those who worked the minerals and created beautiful jewelry and household items, taught their sons to do the same. Farmers trained their sons to care for the land and the animals. Mostly sons took over one set of skills and girls another, though there were no hard and fast rules about this. At twelve years old children needed to choose what they would do. Mostly the girls learnt the spinning and weaving of various cloths, and the art of embroidery. The women made the most wonderful silk cloth, as well as warm woollens for Winter. Sewing and tailoring were the occupations of many women on the Island, but nearly all of them also ran their households. Work in the factories therefore was for half the day only, morning or afternoon.

Pongoland was fairly wealthy because of the quality of its' produce. Some Islands were more artistic or musical. Some tended to have more writers. Each Island hoped to have its' own unique brands, and the Islands bartered their products with each other. The Kings evaluated the products and worked out the relative value of each. They regulated, so to speak, the exchange rates, for purposes of bartering. They each had copies of the fat ledgers they had created containing lists of the values of each item as against the values of the other products in the market. Ledgers were referred to however only in the case of a dispute, because the Islanders themselves had a fine sense of the worth of the things they were exchanging. A little haggling and the issue was usually resolved.

All the Islanders loved concerts and parties, and there were regular get-togethers to which the inhabitants of the neighbouring Islands were invited. The King of Pongoland had instituted an Annual Sports Day for the children of the Islands to compete in. He had learnt about Sports Days from Sonny's description of those held on Earth, and thought them an excellent opportunity for the Island children to learn skills through sports and athletics, while exercising their bodies and keeping fit.

Sonny was excited when he heard about the birthday party. Gogo told him his mother would have his party clothes ready for him when he arrived, and promised to shrink Sonny's present to him to Pongo size.

Sonny's own parents planned to take Sonny to the Zoo as a birthday treat, but that was to take place the week after the Pongoland party. That day Tobo came with Goggles to pick him up and take him back to Pongoland after his Earth bedtime. He had had his usual afternoon sleep. His parents were a little puzzled by this keenness for an afternoon nap but were used to it by now. Tobo sprinkled the usual powdered moss under his bedroom door. The moss gave off an undetectable odour which had the property of inducing forgetfulness. Thus when either of Sonny's parents meant to go into his room, as they approached the door, they forgot why they had meant to go in. The range of the vapour from so small a source was not far. It did not extend to the stairs or into another room, so was harmless.

Tobo's news today was that the King and Queen were to attend the party! Sonny was surprised. Of course Murgo was Chief Minister and close to the King, but that didn't mean usually that the King attended Murgo's children's birthday parties. Goggles greeted Sonny. All the birds of the Islands could talk to some extent and were used to taking messages as well as delivering parcels. Gogo's parents trusted Goggles also to keep an eye on the children and rescue them if need be!

Tobo took Sonny's hand and as he did so Sonny shrank to Gogo's height. The two boys climbed on to Goggles back, and away they flew over the tree-tops and under the stars.

They left our world under a night sky, but as they approached the Islands, the early morning sun was already shining. As Goggles approached Pongoland Sonny could see the green hills and the Palace. Around the other side was the forested hill where Mother Fulati and her daughter Selina lived in their cottage and prepared medicines from the plants growing in their garden. Their house and garden were surrounded by the forest so they had all the ingredients they needed for their work.

The Palace stood at the top of the nearest hill, shining in the golden rays of the dawn sun. Below the Palace were orchards which supplied fruit for the islanders. A winding path led up the hill from the lowland plain to the Palace. Murgo's house was halfway up. The meadow at the bottom of the hill where Goggles now landed was nearly ready for the party. A huge marquee had been erected and inside were a great many little tables and seats. A special large table had been set with a pale gold cloth and that seemed to be the one intended for the Royal Family.

All due respect was paid to the King and Queen as they administered the affairs of the Island. The King stored the Island's supplies of grain, wool, silk, and many other products, ready to be transported as required down to the central market place where there were the Island's shops. There was no money. The supplies belonged to the people. They had been procured in exchange for the merchandise produced by them and brought to the Trade Fair every year. The islanders did keep a certain amount of their own products in their cellars to bring, as individuals, to the Fair for small personal exchanges. For their regular household supplies they went to the market to obtain them from the appropriate shop. No-one horded. No-one cheated. The supplies were there, their own. The exceptions were the very valuble gold and jeweled items. These were of far greater value than the breads and cheeses and household items the islanders bought, and the King used them for the larger purchases for the Island as a whole.

The King also administered justice. There was very little crime, but anyone who had a complaint appeared at the Palace on Court Days. The King interviewed the accused person and decided on the merits of both sides of the argument. Anyone found guilty of harm had to repay in the form of service. On occasion both parties found themselves doing service!

Beyond the respect due to a King and Queen the islanders had a free and easy relationship with the Royal Family. The King and Queen knew them all, and they knew Sonny very well after all the adventures he had been involved in in Pongoland. They treated him as if he was Gogo's brother.

Sonny and Gogo alighted from Goggles' back and set off up the hill to Gogo's house. Its' white gate opened on to the hill path. The walls were painted cream and the roof was red. The boys entered the little garden through the gate and Sonny saw that the house had been decorated with red, yellow, and blue balloons. Mrs Murgo was bustling around adding the final touches to the food she had prepared. Each mother had made things to contribute to the Island's party, but this was her own special feast for her son and Sonny. The Palace had announced that they would contribute the Island's cake. After all it was going to have to be pretty big!

Gogo ran out to meet Sonny and Tobo. He was already dressed in a suit with a gold tunic and red silk trousers. There was also a red silk cap but he didn't have it on. The young people of Pongoland had begun to feel the traditional caps were not cool. The parents sighed and let it go.

"Come on Sonny," he called. "Come and put on you suit!"

Sonny went into the house and through the dining-room where the food was set out, and upstairs to Gogo's bedroom. His party suit was laid out on the bed. His also had a gold tunic but with blue silk trousers and blue cap. Sonny changed into the suit, observing protocol in not putting on the cap. They would take the caps to the party, but put them on only as required. Tobo appeared at the door dressed in a silver-coloured tunic with maroon trousers. As soon as Gogo was ready they went downstairs excitedly. At that moment Murgo came in looking serious. He greeted Sonny and said,

"Come along," he said, "I have brought a carriage to take us up to the Palace."

"What for!" cried Gogo, astonished.

"The King is most anxious to talk to you and Sonny," said Murgo. Sonny's heart missed a beat. Had he done something wrong? Murgo didn't normally look so grave. Oh dear! What could have happened? Tobo started to go with them to the carriage, but Murgo checked him.

"No Tobo. Not today," he said. "The King wishes to talk to Gogo and Sonny alone." Gogo looked frightened! He and Sonny exchanged glances in dismay. Something terrible must have happened!

The carriage belonged to the Palace and had been sent to pick the boys up. They climbed in and set off. It was an open carriage and drawn by two horses, so normally this would have been a wonderful ride in the sunshine, but not today. The journey took only ten minutes, and the carriage went through the gates kept open for them. Then the guards closed them. They alighted and went into the Palace. For a fleeting moment Sonny wondered if he had been taken prisoner! However his common sense reminded him he was in Pongoland to celebrate his birthday, and anyway the King was hardly likely to take a child prisoner. He almost laughed at the thought.

In fact Murgo, Sonny, and Gogo were invited into the King's personal sitting-room, and shortly afterwards the King himself arrived. He was all courtesy and friendliness, and sat down with his three visitors.

"You will be surprised to find yourselves here this morning," he smiled. "I will wish you both happy birthday later on at the party, but there is a subject I wish to discuss with you beforehand. As you know the Queen and I have no children, and you know how important it is for the royal families of the Islands to have a son or daughter to succeed. All the affairs of each Island are known and understood by the Kings and Queens. All the stores, all the account books, all the legal history, and much more are stored in the Palaces. The Kings and Queens are custodians, and they train their heirs to succeed them in the responsibilities of administration. Trade agreements are made between Kings or Queens. Purchases for the whole Island are made by the King or Queen, and as you know of course we have an old established exchange system which is monitored when necessary by the King. A great deal of work is done by the royal families and they in turn rely on the co-operation of the islanders to make sure things run smoothly. See how everyone this very day is participating in the work to make this the best birthday party ever!"

Sonny and Gogo nodded their heads trying to look wise, while wondering why on earth their King should suddenly decide to confide his problems to them! I mean..... what?

"So the point here," said the King, looking at Sonny, "is that I don't have an heir. Sonny I have known you now for four years. I know you to be well-mannered, tactful, courageous, resourceful, and a natural leader. Whatever challenges you have faced while visiting here you have been able to come up with solutions. Shall we ever forget Great-Uncle

Parkin!" The boys smiled. "And you have been able to carry through an enterprise, keeping your mind on the main objective, to a successful conclusion. The qualities I see in you are the qualities I would have wished to find in my own son."

Sonny and Gogo looked beseechingly at Murgo. The King understood their dismay.

"Don't worry Sonny," he reassured him. "You will never be coerced to do anything, or pressured into doing anything which goes against your conscience or wishes. You have your own home, and your own parents, your own world. However I would like you to consider taking the role of a prince here, and of a son to my wife and me. We would train you in all the skills you will need to possess to be a King here one day, and Gogo would always be at your side. The role of Chief Minister is also inherited, and Gogo has always known that one day he will be Chief Minister."

Tears came into Sonny's eyes. King of Pongoland? Him?

"But my parents would never let me!" he cried. "They don't even know I come here! They don't know Pongoland exits!"

"I know," said the King, "and although your visits here have so far been without their knowledge, if you agree to my suggestion you will certainly need to talk to them."

Sonny felt as if the floor was shifting under his feet.

"But how?" he asked.

"We will invite them here for just one visit," said the King. "We will show them round, and let them see what we do, and meet the Islanders."

By now even Gogo was looking confused and upset.

"Your Majesty," he said, "I don't think that will work very well. You haven't met the people of Sonny's world. They haven't any real imagination. They think that what they see and feel is all there is! Once when by accident Sonny's mother saw Pym running along her landing she nearly had a nervous breakdown. And that was because she saw something she didn't believe could happen!"

"I know," said the King, "I really do Gogo. I can in any case allow only one visit. It is their right so it must be. But the dangers of contamination from Earth are real. I have allowed Sonny here because of his nature. But there is a corruption on Earth which I cannot allow here. Because of Sonny I know there must be very many people on Earth like him, but we aren't in a position to investigate all that. As Sonny so often does, we must stick to practicalities."

"So do you mean I would have to live here for ever and never go home?"

"No. You will of course visit your world, and spend time with your parents. And for the next few years you will continue to come here on the same basis, just at the weekend. You must complete your education on Earth, and grow up. Then your parents can explain to people that you have accepted a job abroad. Thousands do. There would be a condition though Sonny. I will need you to marry a Pongo girl. Or possibly, of course, a girl from one of the other Islands. All the Royal Families inter-marry."

"And if I decide not to become a Prince I will be banned from Pongoland?" he cried in horror.

"Not immediately," said the King, "but as you enter your teens you will take on adult concerns and responsibilities. In the end a choice will have to be made. The position is that you are invited to make Pongoland your home, settle here, and become King, or, for the protection of our civilization I should be forced to end the visits. The thought of that saddens me but I too have to make difficult choices."

He saw the looks of hope and horror mixing in the faces of both the boys. He looked at Murgo,

"It is difficult for them to understand," he said.

"I know," said Murgo. "And the challenges?" The King sighed.

"Yes. The challenges. Sonny if you decide to be our King, there will be three tests to be passed. Rites of passage. All princes or princesses destined to be monarch have to complete three tests set by the reigning monarch."

If it were possible Sonny looked even more alarmed.

"What!" he cried.

"Yes, three tests. Knowing you I imagine you will enjoy them, but we won't go into all that until you have made your decision. If you agree to become our King the first step will be to tell your parents about

Pongoland. Then to bring them here to see for themselves. If they agree to my proposition you will start your training here at the weekends. If they do not agree, but you wish to come here eventually, we may have to suspend your visits for a while. Gogo would be with you a lot of the time and keep us posted on how things are going. When you are adult you can make your own decision, but that is a long way off."

"You can take your time, Sonny," said Murgo. "You have until your thirteenth birthday to decide."

"No. Thankyou, Murgo," said Sonny decisively, "I don't need time." He turned to the King.

"The answer is yes, of course. I am already more at home here than on Earth, and often wish I could just stay here. I will talk to my parents, somehow," he looked at Gogo, "with Gogo's advice and suggestions. Please invite them here when you are ready. If they agree I am ready to take the tests whenever you like. If they say no I will finish my education in my world and then come here."

"Well done Sonny," said the King. "We will talk again later, but now I think it is time for us to go to a party!" Sonny stood up and bowed to the King,

"I would like to thank you very much Sir for this huge honour. I will do my very best to prepare myself to serve Pongoland something approaching as well as you do."

The boys left the room. The King turned to Murgo.

"As decisive as ever, even at his age," he smiled. "Those two young men will make a fine team, as we have always been."

As the boys got back into the carriage with Murgo they were very quiet. They had a lot to think about, and they realized their twelfth birthdays would mark the end of their childhood as they had always known it. From now on they would be in training for adulthood. On the one hand this was an exhilarating prospect. On the other hand the safety and careless freedom of early childhood was nearly at an end. Both knew that from now on they would be expected to grow in maturity and wisdom.

Meanwhile preparations for the party in the meadow were nearly completed. Mrs Murgo's jellies, buns, and sandwiches had been collected and taken down to the meadow to set alongside the contributions of all the other mothers. A band had arrived from Meridoland and was already playing background music on the dais. Sonny, Gogo, and Murgo returned to Gogo's house. Mrs Murgo and Tobo were ready and putting last-minute provisions into a bag, so the whole family set off together down the hill on foot.

Sonny and Gogo's spirits lifted immediately. Never mind the cares of the future! Just now it was party day! On a table in the marquee stood the enormous cake sent by the Palace. It was tiered and iced all over in blue with trimmings of green leaves, yellow flowers with tiny orange hearts, and silver lace-work. On top were twenty-four gold candles for two boys aged twelve. Sonny and Gogo gasped, wow!

The guests arrived before the first musical item of the day. This was performed by the Meridoland group called the Spangles. The verses referred to many of the incidents of the past four years in which the boys had come to the aid of an agitated Islander! Everyone laughed and clapped good-naturedly. After that there were games and races for the children. The Queen presented a prize to each winner. The adults sat around in twos and threes on the seats brought to the meadow for the day. When the children seemed to have run off some energy everyone was invited to come into the marquee and serve themselves from the tables which were set out round three sides. The cake was to be cut later. The Meridoland band resumed the background music.

Sonny was haunted again by what the King had said and wandered off with Gogo for a few minutes.

"What do you think Gogo?" he asked anxiously.

"I agree absolutely with your decision. If you don't become King you will have to stop coming here, and that's what I care about. You'll love it!"

"Yes. I think *we* shall love it. My anxiety really is about telling my parents. I sweat to think of it. And how are we to bring them here?"

"By putting them to sleep and carrying them in a blanket? You climbed on to Goggles' back without a second thought but they won't! You will have to introduce the subject though somehow."

"Are you kidding! Tell them casually that they will need to be reduced to the size of garden gnomes to be like everybody else?"

"Yes but Sonny, if we can bring them here asleep they won't know they are the size of garden gnomes will they?"

"Well they will have travelled here by an owl," said Sonny glumly.

"No," said Gogo, "by *four* owls. They will lie on a blanket and be carried by four owls."

"Gogo you have no idea how absolutely crazy this whole thing will be to my parents. They can't think anywhere near big enough."

"No I suppose not. All this seems so normal to us. It *is* normal. We have to think of something plausible."

"And don't forget that my career choice now is to be a King. Not an architect Dad, no. A King. I'll be sitting cosily with a school counselor in no time."

"Sonny I don't think this is going to be for us to work out by ourselves. The King knows how things are, and they will come here by his invitation. Do you think he has no idea how he will get them here? Of course not. We can trust him you know."

"O.K….. Yes. I was having a moment of panic," said Sonny.

The King and Murgo had been watching the boys and noted Sonny's glum face. The King called him over.

"Sonny! Come and walk with me for a minute. You are trying to process the idea of being King here," he said kindly.

"It's not that so much Sir. It's how to tell my parents about Pongoland. I just don't know how to do that."

"We will help you with that," said the King. "The mental gap between our two worlds has to be bridged for them. You know Mother Fulati can prepare all manner of potions, not just to heal the body, but on occasion, when it is deemed necessary, to alter the mind. Gogo has been using that moss regularly for years. Another remedy of hers soothed and reassured your mother the day she saw Pym running about your house. The remedy was essential. She could never have come to terms with what she saw.'

"You mean Mother Fulati could make them something to take the edge off the Pongoland experience?"

The King laughed.

"In all my career she has never let me down," he said. "Whenever I have been faced with some apparently impossible situation she has come to my rescue. I trust her completely."

"I would be so grateful Sir. I trust her too."

"Leave it to me. Grown-up worries have to be dealt with by adults. Let's forget all that for today, and I will ask for Mother Fulati's help. The incredible must appear normal. She will devise something so don't worry."

Chapter Two

Sonny's Parents Learn the Truth

The next week went by as usual in Sonny's home. He went to school, did his homework, played with his friends, and watched TV – which by now was available all night! But his parents noticed he was preoccupied. The following Sunday they took him to the Zoo, and they had a wonderful family day out. Sonny's main present was a new bicycle and he nearly cried. His parents were so good to him! At least until he was eighteen he would carry on as before while he underwent his training in Pongoland at the weekends.

That very night Gogo arrived on Goggles carrying a green bottle and Goggles was waiting on the neem tree. However Sonny had not rested in the afternoon and had school the next day, so could not go to Pongoland.

"That's OK," said Gogo. "Let's just talk."

They sat on Sonny's bed and Gogo uncorked the green bottle for a moment, and closed it again.

"We mustn't breathe this," he said. "It's the stuff for your parents from Mother Fulati."

"So I have to hold my breath as I ask my parents to sniff it?"

"No! Just hide it somewhere. It's to let them breathe when they travel to Pongoland, so that Pongoland will look OK. We'll be outside on Goggles' back in the fresh air so it won't affect us."

"Right. Is there anything for when I have to tell them about Pongoland in the first place?"

"For that I've got some drops," said Gogo, taking a little bottle from his pocket. It became six inches long for Sonny's world. He held it sideways and showed it to Sonny. Inside was a little model ship, perfectly fashioned. Sonny exclaimed in wonder.

"Yes, it's lovely. When the liquid has evaporated they might like to put it on display. The thing is you get it out to show them when you get to the subject of Pongoland. You can tell them that this is from Pongoland, and, (having taken off the stopper), encourage them to look inside to see the workmanship close to. They will then automatically breathe in the vapour. Keep talking. Tell them you have been invited to succeed as King there. There will have been a slight opening of their consciousness. That will allow what you say to be at least partially understood. Then that same night we will take them to Pongoland."

"Alright," said Sonny dubiously. "Could it be next Saturday night then? And I will talk about Pongoland just before bed-time."

"Fine. I will go home now, but I will come back tomorrow for the week so that I can keep everyone informed there, and let them know if there are any snags," said Gogo.

Sonny laughed dolefully.

"It's all snag Gogo," he said.

Gogo returned the following morning to spend the week with Sonny. On Wednesday Sonny asked,

"Please would you take me to meet Mother Fulati tonight? I think I need to discuss with her myself the effects of the potions."

"Of course," said Gogo.

They left a little earlier than usual so that Sonny could be back in bed in fairly good time. Today they passed over the meadow and headed straight to the forests on the slope of the farther hill where Mother Fulati's house could be seen in a clearing. The house was surrounded by a very large garden in which there were tree-lined paths, and many beds for flowering plants and herbs. They landed on her lawn. The jackdaws and crows in her trees started up a ruckus and her cat disappeared round the back of the house. Mother Fulati herself came out of the kitchen on to her small patio, her arms outstretched to greet them. She hugged them and ushered them into her house. Before they could say

15

a word she made them sit at her table and gave them each hot buttered scone. She was said to be of ancient gypsy stock, and unlike the other people of Pongoland she wore a long full skirt to her ankles with a short blouse fitted into the waist. Her hair was full length and knotted at the back of her head. Her daughter Selina smiled at them but she was up to her elbows in flour as she kneaded dough for bread. There was a large kitchen range for the many remedies and potions which had to be brewed every day. They served neighbouring Islands as well as their own people, so this work never stopped. Things were merely left on hold at night.

"Now what can I do for you?" she asked. "I have heard your news Sonny and I am delighted. You must have a lot of questions though."

"Yes I have Mother Fulati, but right now I wondered if you could tell me a bit more about the potions you have sent for my parents. What actually will they do?"

"Of course," she said. "You are a good sensible boy not to want to treat your parents with medicines you don't understand. We can't just call a thing magic without understanding what that means. You know that people flying in aeroplanes from you world never encounter these Islands. The reason is, as probably you have been told, that they exist in higher dimension."

"Yes," said Sonny, "and I have heard about people and planes apparently disappearing into another dimension."

"That may or not be true," said Mother Fulati, "but everything vibrates, you see. Everything in creation vibrates, but at different speeds. You can't see a level of creation which vibrates at a different speed from yours. Our Islands exist on a slightly higher plane from yours."

"I see," said Sonny, and he did, "but I must vibrate at the speed of my own world, and Gogo and Tobo, and even Murgo once, visit my world without disappearing."

"Yes," said Mother Fulati. "They belong to the family of Murgo Pongo and going back into our most ancient history they, and the King, have always had the ability to cross dimensions. They have the ability to slow down or speed up at will. No-one else can do that unless conducted by one of his family. One day Gogo, as a young child, wandered across dimensions into your world and met you. Instinctively he knew how to transmit the energy necessary for you to become his height, and bring you here. You were also a young child living still in the imagination. Alice in Wonderland changed sizes, so there you were, doing the same. You thought nothing of climbing on to Goggles' back. It was that child's faith which enabled you to return here with Gogo. Normally no-one from another dimension is allowed here, but the King recognized that unique faith in you and didn't want to stifle your gift. You proved discreet and an excellent friend. At any moment the King could have asked Murgo's family not to return to your house, but he never did."

"Right. OK," said Sonny.

"My Dad taught me about crossing dimensions when I was quite small. Tobo was also taught. We had to know how to get back, you see, if we drifted, and it was easy for us to drift. Normally I see a place in my mind's eye, and fix it with an intention to get there, and I do. My first trip to your world was accidental somehow."

"How do you make me small?" asked Sonny.

"It's also done in the mind. In your world you can enlarge or contract photos very easily. It's the same process. Big Sonny, little Sonny."

"I get that but I don't think I'll ever grasp how," said Sonny. "But these potions, Mother Fulati. They are to confuse reality and fantasy in my parents' minds. Is that so?"

"They speed up the vibrational rate just a little to bring into focus things which otherwise would be beyond the person's imagination and rejected. The result is that when you describe Pongoland to them they will be able to see it in their mind's eye in the same they would be able to visualise a place in your own world. The vapour from the liquid in the larger bottle for the journey is a bit stronger to lift them into Pongoland comfortably. The effect will wear off soon but by then they will have seen that Pongoland is real. The effects from both preparations are very short-lived."

"Alright, thanks," said Sonny. "The other thing is that they will arrive in Pongoland in nightie and pyjamas! Never mind Pongoland my parents would be dismayed!"

"You are so compassionate, my child," said Mother Fulati, smiling, "understanding their mortification, but the King and Queen will be in the meadow to meet them, and will have beautiful clothes for them to put on immediately. They will take them home with them as keepsakes, and as proofs later that they really did come here."

By Saturday morning Sonny felt sick with nerves, but there was no going back. Soon before he was due to go to bed he said brightly,

"I've been thinking about what I want to do when I grow up."

"Oh?" said his mother.

"Yes. I want to be a King," he said firmly. His father laughed.

"Seriously," Sonny persevered. "Imagine being King of a country where people live in peace and harmony, where there is no traffic, no pollution, and where everyone has enough to eat and a house to live in."

"If you become King of a country like that, I shall come and live there," his father joked.

"Ah, but no traffic?" said his mother. "Presumably you would have electricity?" she asked, playing along.

"Electricity yes, but no TV or radio Mum. Lots of sunshine to do things outside. Everything hand-made, and an economy based on a barter system. Beautiful countryside. Lots of music, art, and literature, but no money."

"Well," said his father, smiling, "you've certainly got it worked out. You must write a novel about that. However societies like that no longer exist, probably never did. There has always been exploitation."

"Not with a good King in charge," persisted Sonny. He looked so earnest his parents began to look at him seriously. This was the moment to produce the ship!

"See what a friend gave me!" he said proudly, giving it to his father. Both his parents exclaimed. The workmanship was so perfect!

"You can take out the cork to get a closer look," said Sonny. His father took removed the cork stopper and peered into the bottle to see the details of the ship. Then he handed it to his mother, and she too had a close look. They discussed the minute carving of the hull and the tiny details of the deck, but his father said,

"I don't think you can keep this Sonny. Do your friend's parents know he has given it away? I'm sure he was not meant to do that."

"No. It's alright Dad. But I will give it back. I just wanted you to see it first."

"It's perfect," said his mother." It must have been very expensive."

This was his moment.

"No Mum. It was bartered for some medicines. Mother Fulati exchanged herbal medicines in exchange for the ship."

"Wh….what?" said his father.

"In the kingdom I was telling you about, Pongoland." His parents gaped, but the vapour was beginning to have its' effect.

"Pongoland is an Island in the sky. It's one of an archipelago of islands which exist in the sky about half an hour from Earth, owl-time."

"Islands in the sky?" said his mother. "But planes fly in and out of airports all the time. No-one has noticed any islands."

"We have a moon circling the Earth and there's a space-station," said his father. "We are observing the universe all the time, and no-one has seen them."

"No," said Sonny, and going the whole hog while the vapour lasted. "They exist in a different dimension from ours of course, so they are invisible from our dimension. Each Island has a King, and the Islands live as I have been describing. Pongoland's First Minister is Murgo Pongo. Members of his family have inherited the gift of being able to cross dimensions, so one day four years ago, Murgo's son Gogo came to visit Earth and met me. He came here. The islanders fly on birds to visit each other, and Gogo came on his family's bird, an owl called Goggles."

His parents just stared at him.

"So one night," he pressed on, "Gogo took me back to his home in Pongoland. When Gogo holds my hand he transmits some energy, light energy I think, to me and reduces me to his height, which is small. We climb on Goggles' back and off we go!"

"When?" asked his mother.

"In the night, Mum. I come back before morning. We have had so many wonderful adventures in Pongoland. It's a lovely place."

"Every night?" asked his father.

"No. Just at the weekends. That's why I take an afternoon nap."

"So Gogo comes for you on Goggles' back," said his mother.

"Yes, that's right, but a lot of the time Gogo stays here with me during our day. Daytime here is night-time there, so he sleeps on my bed. He's that puppet-doll, except he's not a puppet. He keeps still while you're around so as not to frighten you."

"But he's what? Fifteen inches tall!" said his father.

"Sixteen inches now to be exact. He has been growing, but so slowly you wouldn't notice. And so am I when he takes my hand. He contracts me like we can contract photographs. It's some light process Dad."

He left his account at that, feeling he had better just let it sink in while they were under the influence of the vapour. Gogo and he were to take them to Pongoland tonight, and they would see for themselves. At present they were in a state of suspended disbelief. He hoped they wouldn't be frightened, but Pongoland would be like some perfect holiday resort in their eyes, and he thought they would love it!

Gogo was waiting anxiously in his bedroom, and listened to Sonny's report.

"So, not too bad so far?" he said.

"No," said Sonny. "That medicine helped enormously. It meant they listened quietly and asked sensible questions. They are feeling sleepy now, so hopefully will soon go to bed."

They did indeed. Sonny went to check after some time, and reported to Gogo that they were asleep. Gogo signalled to Goggles who was waiting on the nearby tree along with eight more Pongoland owls. Tobo had brought them through and was directing them. He came to Sonny's windowsill on Goggles back carrying two large sheets. Gogo took them from him and all the boys went into Sonny's parents' room. Gogo took Sonny's father's hand, and Tobo took his mother's hand, and they were reduced to the size of Pongo adults, in the region of two feet tall, his mother a bit less. The boys then gently lifted them on to a sheet each. Tobo sat beside his mother on her sheet. Goggles brought the other owls, and they lifted the sheets, an owl to each corner. They held the corners firmly and carried them out through their window. The owls were well accustomed to carrying both people and merchandise in this manner. Sonny and Gogo climbed on to Goggles' back and off they all flew, over the tree-tops and under the stars. Tobo spent some time allowing Sonny's mother to breathe the vapour from the larger bottle. Then he signaled to Sonny's father's owls, and climbed on to his sheet. He then allowed him to breathe the vapour for a while too. Sonny felt he needed a whiff of the vapour himself, so extraordinary were the events of the night!

As they approached Pongoland the early morning sun was shining down on the green meadow. It was a beautiful day with the scents of many blossoms in the air, and the greens of the hills and the forest all around. The Palace at the top of the nearest hill shone pale gold in the sunlight, and all the little houses on the hillside looked bright and homely. Each tiny garden was in bloom, and a lot of people were out already doing their early morning chores.

The owls laid the two sheets gently on the grass. Murgo and his wife were waiting for them. They had a jug of fresh juice to revive Sonny's parents, and a set of clothes for each, as well as Sonny's own blue and cream suit kept at Gogo's house. Sonny quietly changed into his clothes and knelt by his parents to wake them. They felt the ground beneath them and awoke startled. They felt the soft breeze and wondered for a moment if they were on holiday. They sat up and Mrs Murgo stepped forward with a large glass of juice for each. They were thirsty from the effects of the vapour and drank it all. They took in the sight of Sonny in his blue tunic and cream trousers, and recognized Gogo as the "doll" Sonny had had on his bed for so long. He smiled at them.

"So….where are we?" asked Sonny's father.

"In Pongoland Dad," said Sonny. "We thought you would like to come and see for yourselves. It's nice isn't it?"

Murgo and Mrs Murgo introduced themselves, and Sonny's parents, apart from a greeting, remained quiet. Sonny said,

"Look Mum, these are some clothes for you to wear for today. Tonight we will take you home."

"Oh, thankyou, but darling how did we get here? Don't tell me this is your Island in the sky and we have crossed dimensions!"

"Yes it is Mum. Owls brought you here on these sheets. Look there they are having their breakfast." The owls were tucking into bowls of food provided by Murgo.

"They're pretty big," said Sonny's father. "Much bigger than ours."

"Yes they are," said Sonny. "They are the Island's transport." Mrs Murgo said,

"If you would like to dress behind those bushes we'll take you to our home for breakfast. Then we will show you the Island."

Sonny's parents were bereft of speech really, and quietly did as suggested. His father was given maroon and white, and his mother yellow and dark brown. Sonny felt they would not want to wear the hats so just carried them. They set off up the hill to Gogo's house, making polite conversation about the weather and the scenery. They were long past surprise. They found Gogo's house homely and beautiful with polished furniture, decorative wool rugs, and gleaming bronze and silver-ware. The kitchen dresser was like their own with the crockery stacked on it. Breakfast was ready in the kitchen and they sat down to a cereal, egg, and toast and marmalade. They talked about the house, and about Gogo and Tobo's school as compared to Sonny's.

A simple carriage with two horses had been sent down from the Palace to take them up the hill to visit the King and Queen, and then to take them round the Island, so after breakfast they set off to meet the King and Queen. A royal guard met them at the gate, and another official came out to conduct them in to the King's personal sitting-room. There the King and Queen were waiting for them.

"I hope you are adjusting comfortably to this experience," said the King. "You will be back home again this evening, but we hope you will enjoy your day with us here, and take back memories of this world to your own. I think you will notice that our life-style is very simple. I have visited your world so do know something about it. Our civilization is more advanced in some ways. We can make things happen without the machinery you employ, and we are advanced in the uses of herbs and plants for medication. You will see something of that. Sonny tells me you are keen gardeners so I think you would enjoy a visit to Mother Fulati and a walk round her garden. Then our hills here are rich in minerals and you would probably like to see the men at work there fashioning beautiful things. Our women make fine cloths of silk and wool, and are artists in embroidery."

"Thankyou Sir, Ma'am," said Sonny's father. "We look forward to seeing your beautiful Island."

The tour went ahead and Sonny's parents had a truly wonderful day. They had lunch at the Palace and tea back at Murgo's house. As expected they were especially delighted with Mother Fulati's garden and talked with her a lot about her preparations. As they arrived back at Murgo's house, Sonny's father said,

"So what is this about you becoming King here, Sonny?" Murgo heard him.

"After tea John, the King will come to discuss that with you. He wanted you to look round, and meet us first. Now he will put to you his proposition," said Murgo.

The King arrived at five o'clock and was taken into Murgo's sitting-room. There he outlined for Sonny's parents the life and responsibilities Sonny would have on the Island, first as Prince and later succeeding as King."

"But Sonny is a human boy!" cried Sonny's mother. "What does he know about the way you do things here?"

"He knows us very well. Gogo would be his Chief Minister and attend to all the things that might be difficult for Sonny, as Murgo does for me. Sonny's job would be administration. He would look after supplies, and learn about how much of what is needed for imports and how much of what to export. He would mete out justice and he would handle all the diplomatic affairs of the Island. He would be responsible for the well-being of the people and attend to any matters of concern. In all these areas I believe Sonny to be well-qualified. Management is a practical business and he is deeply practical."

"Of course we have always said that he will be free to make his own career choice, but had never dreamt of anything like this," said his father. "Myself I shan't oppose it. But we will need to talk with Sonny a lot about what leaving our world and living here is going to mean."

"In any case he will live with you at home until he has finished his schooling. I wondered if you might tell people then that he has accepted a job abroad? There will be no restrictions about visiting you of course. The only condition I would make is that he marry a girl from one of our Islands."

"What do you think, Jane?" asked Sonny's father.

"I know he has a good mind and a compassionate heart and I think he could do this, but he shouldn't make a hasty decision. He has eight years left yet of education. He must apply himself as well as if he were planning to go to University in our world. If he continues to want to settle here then so be it," she said.

They had heard and seen as much as they take in for the time being, so Goggles was called to come with the other owls to take them home. The visit had been very pleasurable to Sonny's parents in spite of feeling dazed by it all. Their night clothes were folded up and ready for them to take back, and soon they were on their way. Gogo and Sonny travelled with them and Gogo restored them and all the clothes to Earth size. Then Gogo returned to Pongoland with the owls. Very tired by now, Sonny and his parents got back into bed and were asleep in no time.

Chapter Three

The Ring of the Dragon's Hair

During the next week Sonny's parents talked long and hard with Sonny about his future. They remembered every detail of their day in Pongoland clearly, and how normal and happy it had all seemed. They had the gifts from the miners and the cloth mills, enlarged to the correct size for their world, to show for their adventure. But the idea that they had "crossed a dimension", and that Pongoland was as real as this world, was hard to digest once they were back in their own home.

Sonny did not argue. He listened to all they said about the future which lay before him in his own world, and the sacrifices he would have to make to live in Pongoland. He understood all that fully. His only real argument against what his parents said was that he wanted to live in Pongoland. The very idea of not being able to go back there was too scary to contemplate.

Gogo lay in his bed all day and Sonny's parents got used to the idea that he was sleeping, not inanimate. Every evening Sonny and Gogo talked until Sonny fell asleep. Then Gogo went home for the night. On Friday night he took Sonny with him. He did not put any moss powder under the door because his parents would know where he was.

The King was keen that Sonny should go to the Palace so that he and the Queen could discuss the future. Murgo and Gogo and Tobo went with him. They were all exceedingly happy to hear that he would live in Pongoland eventually.

The King raised the subject of the three tests Sonny would undergo.

"The first test is mainly of resourcefulness," he said, "I know of course that you have plenty of that quality, but the test I am going to set you may be beyond your power to fulfil."

"I can only do my best, Sir," said Sonny anxiously.

"I don't suppose you have heard of the Ring of the Dragon's Hair have you?" asked the King.

"No Sir," said Sonny.

"It has belonged to the King of Meridoland for centuries. It is inherited by each succeeding King, and worn on the left hand. Unfortunately the current King has just lost it."

"Oh no!" cried the three boys, horrified.

"Yes," said the King, "and you would do the very greatest favour to the King of Meridoland, his wife, Lord Lannet and Princess Ahoosti if you could restore it to them. Otherwise he will go down in history as the King who lost the Ring of Dragon's Hair. It won't matter what his other achievements are. That is what will be remembered."

"They must have looked for it everywhere themselves. They do seem to keep losing things! It was a coronet last time!" said Sonny. The King smiled.

"Yes, though that wasn't really their own fault. The history of the ring is a great deal more important than the ring. It is indeed a very fine thing, made of gold with a dragon's head breathing fire crafted from ruby, amber, and quartz. It commemorates an event which took place so far back in history no-one can remember it, apart from what the ring signifies. In those very olden times there were dragons. A King had to defend his people against evil monsters, sorcery, and witch-craft. Those were dangerous times before the people of these islands learnt never ever to use magic against each other. It always bounces back on the attacker. Always. It took centuries for people to understand that. Evil as well as good is a boomerang. One day a wise old hermit told the King that in order to render their Dragon powerless he must steal a hair from its' tail. The tail of the Dragon was long and very powerful and the Dragon hardly ever slept."

Sonny, Gogo, and Tobo were listening to the story with eyes like saucers.

"So what did he do?" asked Gogo.

"Well a King has to save and protect his people, and if necessary lay down his life for them. So he knew he had no choice. The wise old hermit gave the King a sword to conquer the Dragon, but the Dragon was thirty feet long, the sword was three feet long, and the King was six feet tall."

"What happened?" asked Tobo.

"It was a long and arduous expedition, and every Island has the Chronicles of the Kings of Maridoland in its' library if you wish to read it. The upshot was that the King found a good witch living in a cave who made powerful magic potions. In return for a promise that she and her female descendents would always hold a high rank in the kingdom as healers, she made him a sleeping draft so strong that it could put to sleep a herd of elephants. Armed with a vial of this brew the King approached the Dragon in the dead of night. He crept up to the Dragon treading very softly. As he grew near to its' nose it reared its' head in alarm. It opened its' mouth to engulf the King in flames, but before it could do so the King tossed the vial straight into its' throat. The Dragon breathed in the fumes and sank into a deep sleep. Immediately the King leapt round to the back of the Dragon, seized a hair in his fist, and pulled it out! The old hermit gave the ring to the King of Meridoland in perpetual memory of the feat of wisdom and courage he had displayed to save his Island. The story has been an inspiration to every King since, and a lesson in what kingship means."

"And what of the wise woman? Meridoland doesn't have a good witch now," said Sonny.

"No but Pongoland does, and we are not so far away. Who knows what happened in all the succeeding centuries? Many people believe that at some stage a descendent of that original good witch migrated to Pongoland and our Mother Fulati is the current wise woman. She does hold an important rank on our Island," said the King. "I never challenge her."

"How interesting," breathed Sonny. "So it is really important that we find this ring!"

"It is," said the King, "and that is your first assignment. You will need to arrange to come here for a few days to fulfil it, if you can. You wouldn't be able to do it in one day. Don't get confused Sonny. I am not sending you into danger! I wouldn't dream of it. You are children. This is an exercise for your wits. The whole of Meridoland has been scouring the Island for that ring. Gogo will of course go with you."

Tobo was a mature little boy by now, and understood he could not take part in these tests. He promised plenty of advice though before they set off! Everyone laughed.

"Any advice you can give us will be greatly appreciated Tobo," said Sonny hugging him.

The King looked on approvingly. It was this unfailing kindness in Sonny that was in the King's eyes his chief qualification to rule his beloved Island.

"Sir, I have a question," said Sonny, "how is it the people of the Islands speak English?"

"Ah," said the King, "there is a belief that one of the Knights of King Arthur of England strayed across the dimensions into ours. Theirs is a very mystical story you know, the story of King Arthur, and the twelve Knights, and the Round Table. All those Knights went on missions and had adventures. It is believed one of them came here in a dream and explored our Islands. Originally the peoples of the Islands spoke different languages, but we all learnt English from him. Then we retained English as our common language. It is even rumoured that Mother Fulati's ancestry goes back to that Knight. You know she looks and dresses differently from the rest of us."

"What!!" exclaimed Sonny. "But what about size differences?"

"Oh come Sonny," smiled the King, "where is your sense of magic? Maybe Murgo's ancestry goes back to that time too to give him the 'touch'?" Sonny laughed.

"Yes of course. Who am I to talk about impossibilities?"

"Quite. An open mind here is polite! Our Kings even acknowledge an allegiance to King Arthur. Some even believe the wise old hermit who gave the King of Meridoland the sword was Merlin. Whatever the reality every new King here goes on a pilgrimage to Camelot. I told you

I visited your world once. I went to Camelot. The traditions of honour and chivalry taught by King Arthur we also observe."

"So," said the essentially practical Sonny, "your English has been updated regularly because the Kings of the Islands go to Camelot?" The King smiled.

"Yes, and we also have old books from England in our libraries, reduced in size of course. There's a lot for you to study Sonny. These islands have a rich history, and much culture. But go now and enjoy yourselves. Your test can be done when you can arrange to come here for three or four days."

In the end it was agreed that Sonny should come to Pongoland for his half-term holiday. He and Gogo and Tobo were elated, no matter what the reason, though not so elated when the King said Sonny must sleep at the Palace when not away on another Island.

"He needs to become very familiar with the Palace and how things work here," he said when the boys arrived to see him. "I have written to the King of Meridoland to let him know you will be coming today to look for the ring. You and Gogo will stay in his Palace. I have explained that this is one of your tests as heir to my throne."

"O.K.," said Sonny feeling very awkward, "I mean thankyou Sir. Shall we ask Goggles to take us?"

"Goggles can indeed take you but escorted by one of my personal owls. This is an official visit."

Sonny had lunch at Mrs Murgo's house and after that he and Gogo went down to the meadow. The King was there with his owl called Ben and he saw them off with good wishes and blessings.

They arrived after about half an hour. Meridoland was a mountainous island with deep valleys, and caverns hollowed out in the hillsides. There were plateaus also where people met each other for parties or other festivities. The King's Palace had been built at the top of the highest mountains, and the owls drew in to land in its' courtyard. Sonny had been to Meridoland twice before and knew the Royal Family. The King and Queen came out to meet them. They enjoyed the idea that one of Sonny's tests was to find their ring!

"This is going to be a really difficult task Sonny," said the King. "We have so many mountains and ravines, so if for instance the ring was dropped down one of them you really have no chance of finding it."

"No I expect not Sir," said Sonny, "but how could that happen? Our King says it is always on your finger." The Queen sighed.

"That is true,' she said, "but when we went to bed one Sunday night it was safe on his finger, I know for sure. When we woke up in the morning it was gone! Someone stole it. We haven't just lost it."

"So say if it was thrown off a mountain-top, that would be as a punishment or out of revenge wouldn't it?" suggested Sonny.

"Yes but this is a very difficult thing someone did, to take it off my finger in the night! There are other ways of punishing me if someone felt badly treated. And I can't for the life of me think who!"

"The ring is so ancient, Sonny," said the Queen, "that it is believed to have magical properties. Some think Merlin gave it to the King's ancestor, and he was a wizard, a seer."

"What sort of properties?" asked Sonny.

"Well," said the King, "someone might think it has healing properties. It is believed to confer energy and grace on the wearer, and the monarch will commune with it before any enterprise of great importance. One King did that long ago before a battle with the Toliks, before we learnt how to negociate agreements fairly. And as it happened Meridoland won, but I think nowadays no-one would like to say that was because of the ring!"

"But nowadays also everyone goes to Mother Fulati for healing. That would be far easier and better than stealing a ring off your finger in the night! Who would risk stealing such a famous ring when all they have to do is fly to Pongoland?"

"I know," said the King. "We are clutching at straws here."

"We have wracked our brains as to who might want to steal the ring for what, and have come up with no answers," said the Queen. "Anyway come in and have some refreshments and I will show you your room. Then the two of you can proceed as you like."

"Everyone has been instructed to help you or answer any questions," said the King.

"Thankyou Sir," said Gogo, "how are Lord Lannet and Princess Ahoosti?"

"They are very well and will meet you later," smiled the Queen.

The Meridos were of the same height as the Pongos, but usually had darker curly hair. The Pongos had brown hair and pointed noses. There was a certain amount of inter-marrying between the islanders so racial characteristics were blurred sometimes. The two boys went into the lobby of the Palace and were served lemonade, and after that they were taken up to their room in one of the Palace towers. It had windows all round and magnificent views across the mountains from all of them. Two beds were made up with primrose coloured quilts, and on the floor were two crimson rugs. Sonny and Gogo just had one bag containing a night-shirt each and a change of clothes. A window seat ran all round the room so they went to sit on it and look outside.

"It really is a puzzle," said Gogo. "Where do we start?"

"Well it might be an idea to ask around to find out if anyone is in any sort of trouble, and possibly thinks the ring could help," suggested Sonny. "We need to wander around generally I think and try to spot anything odd."

"You mean any sort of odd?" said Gogo.

"Yes I think we have to find something which is different from usual. People know where the ring is Gogo. It was taken at great risk, and I believe we can assume it is hidden somewhere. It hasn't been thrown away when it is believed to have magical properties."

"You're right!" said Gogo.

"You remember that plateau where we all met together at the time of Lannet and Ahoosti's marriage? Let's start there. It seemed to be a general sort of meeting-place, and we could mooch around there chatting generally and keeping our eyes open."

"And our ears close to the ground," said Gogo.

They went down the winding stairs in the tower which led to their room, and along a corridor. Then down some more stairs to a back door. They crossed a small courtyard, and took a path which led down to the plateau. They were familiar with area because of having been guests at the wedding. It was a fine walk down the mountain-side. They passed the place where Tobo had had a fall, and soon after reached the plateau. Several Merido children were running up and down and playing ball. A group of women occupied a wooden seat overlooking the valley. Some men were approaching by a path which led up the hill. There were farms dotted over the hillside, and these kept sheep and goats mainly, but some cows. Down in the valley there were fields of corn, and a tractor could be seen at work.

Sonny and Gogo took another seat and waited to see if anyone would approach them. The children did immediately, so Sonny and Gogo greeted them in a friendly way asking if this was a school holiday. The children were curious about them. They recognized Gogo as from Pongoland, but asked Sonny where he was from. The boys chatted with them asking where they lived, and if the women close by were their mothers. After a few minutes they remarked that they were looking for the King's ring. Gogo asked if they had any idea where it might be. The children shuffled their feet as if they feared they were being accused of having something to do with its' loss.

"No we don't think that *you* have it of *course*," reassured Sonny. "You would definitely give it back to the King immediately. We just wondered if you have any ideas, that's all."

"There's an old man," offered an older boy wearing a red cap. "He walks funny and he talks to himself."

"Oh," said Gogo, "that does sound odd, but maybe he's just not very well. Only a fit person could have the ring." Sonny and Gogo had agreed not to discuss any of the details about the loss, so that they could guage the truth of what anyone else might say.

"We are all very fit," said a little girl laughing. "We run up and down the mountain all the time!"

"Even right to the top where the Palace is?" said Sonny. "That is very high."

"If we want," said the girl. "We come here to play after school, or at the weekends. Our houses are along that path." She pointed across the hill road to a path which led off round the mountain.

"Where does that path lead?" asked Gogo.

"All the way round the mountain," said another boy aged about ten. "Sometimes we have races round it to see who can do it the fastest!"

"That's for the grown-ups though," said the first boy. "It's too far for children either to walk or run."

"What is there round the other side?" asked Sonny. "Are there caves or streams or what?"

"No caves!" said the little girl laughing again. "There is a stream, and you can climb up or down beside it to a few farms. Sometimes we go for picnics round there with our parents. We can take a pony and cart along the main path and then walk."

"Sounds nice," said Sonny. "Do you go down to the valley much?"

Seeing the children all talking and being friendly with the newcomers, the women came across to meet them, and heard the question.

"Those of us who live up the mountain-side don't go down to the valley very often because it is such a steep climb back. Even the ponies don't like the climb. Sometimes we go."

"What is there down there?" asked Gogo.

"Two or three arable farms, and there is the town. We go into town once a month by pony-trap for shopping."

"We are here to help the King find his lost ring," said Sonny.

"Oh?" said one of the women. They too looked defensive as if afraid someone might accuse them. Perhaps everyone felt suspect until it was found.

"It's alright, honestly, the King doesn't suspect any of you of course. But someone has it you know. Someone close to the Palace." The women relaxed enough to show their own anxiety.

"That ring is very important to all of us on the Island," said one of them.

"I know," said Sonny. "We do hope we can be of help. Are there any clues?"

"No......," said another, "only that the next day, after the ring disappeared there was a weird light in the sky."

"What?" exclaimed Sonny. "What sort of light?"

"As if an angel was going to appear," said the woman, "but then disappeared again."

"Where?" asked Gogo.

"Over the Palace," said the woman, "Merlin himself gave that ring to the King's ancestor, so maybe Merlin was angry."

"No," said Sonny, "surely not angry. The King has not dishonoured the ring."

"But supposing someone else did?" suggested another woman.

"Dishonoured how?" asked Gogo.

"Dishonoured it by using it as it isn't supposed to be used," said an old woman in the group. "It isn't supposed to be used for magic. Merlin warned that. He said if it was needed for good purposes, the King would receive energy from the ring without even having to ask for it. But if a King ever wanted power from it for a bad purpose the ring would punish." The women fell silent. They were uneasy.

"So you wonder if maybe someone has got it for a bad purpose?" asked Sonny.

"Maybe," said the old woman. The women turned to go, calling the children after them as it was time for tea.

"Weird," commented Gogo.

"Yeah. I mean what possible bad purpose could anyone have on Meridoland?"

"No idea. Think of Pongoland. We had Toplo and his ridiculous bonka. He even captured the Spangles, but he was just silly really. He didn't mean anyone any real harm," said Gogo.

"Well what about Lord Lannet. He and the Princess will rule the Island after her parents. Might there be anyone here who minds that?"

Gogo was uneasy.

"These are bad thoughts Sonny," he said.

"I know Gogo, and we won't say a single word of this to anyone else, but maybe between the two of us we should explore the possibility?"

"I think there was another lord who had wanted to marry Princess Ahoosti, but she chose Lord Lannet." They pondered for a moment.

"O.K.," said Sonny, "who was that?"

"Er......Sesko........Sisko. Sisko it was. Lord Sisko. He lives somewhere to the North of here."

"Well, just in *case*, I think we should find out where. Don't let's mention it in the Palace and cause a hullaballoo there, but tomorrow morning let's ask for a pony and trap to take us down to the town. We can ask around there, and find out how to get to his house."

"Castle. He lives in a castle. He's quite wealthy I believe. His family is very distantly related to the Royal Family."

"And he expected maybe to marry Ahoosti and become King?" said Sonny.

"Yes, probably," said Gogo.

"So what has changed? Why now? I mean supposing he's got the ring."

"Sonny he might even feel the ring should be his. You know how sometimes there is more than one valid candidate to succeed as King. In that case the Islanders vote. Whoever they choose is crowned."

"Did that happen, say, with Sisko's father at all?"

"Not that I know of, but there might have been bad feeling. Or Sisko just wanted to share the throne by marrying Ahoosti, supposing he's involved, which we don't know."

"No, but let's make that our investigation tomorrow," said Sonny.

"We're always getting involved in these big messes, and we are children," grumbled Gogo.

"All the same we have done O.K. Gogo. Cheer up," grinned Sonny.

The next morning, on their request, a pony and trap arrived for Sonny and Gogo after breakfast. They could ask Goggles to take them, but they wouldn't see anything from his back. Gogo was used to driving one so he took the driver's seat, and they set off down the hill to the town. The King and Queen were not surprised that they should wish to go there, and they told the boys about the town and the routes leading from it. Sonny and Gogo asked the useful questions about the area without betraying that they intended to go to Lord Sisko's Castle. It would have been helpful to learn more about him but not so good to raise suspicions against him.

The day was beautiful as days usually were in the Islands. The journey down the hill took about forty-five minutes, so they would need to allow an hour to return up it. The little town was already quite busy. The shops were opening and people were setting off to work. They took the pony and cart to an Inn the King had told them about. They went inside and found themselves in a large room in which small tables were arranged, each with a coloured cloth. Sonny and Gogo chose one with a green cloth, and a young Merido girl came to ask them what they would like. Gogo asked for two glasses of mixed fruit juice. When she left them to get the drinks Sonny muttered,

"Somehow we have to get into conversation. We need to know more about Sisko without introducing his name if we can."

"We can try to get her to talk about the sights on the Island," said Gogo, so when she returned with two glasses of pink fruit juice on a little tray he said,

"We wondered if you could suggest places for us to visit this morning? I am from Pongoland and this is my friend. We have a pony and trap and would like to visit some of the interesting places in Meridoland."

The girl put down the tray. She wore a blue uniform dress with a white apron. In its' pocket she carried a note-pad and pencil for taking orders.

"O.K.," she said, "would you like to look at the countryside, or are you more interested in historical places?"

"Er.....what historical places could you suggest?" asked Sonny.

"We've got a Wishing-Well," she said with a smile. "People usually like to go there. You drop a pebble into it and make a wish. That is up a hill-side. A little stream trickles down the hill and long ago the Well was built into the hill so that water would run into it. People believe that the wizard Merlin built it and blessed the stream, but I'm not sure that is true!"

"All the same we'ld love to make a wish," said Gogo, laughing. "Is there anything else interesting to see in the same area?"

"Er, well, you can go on up the hill. You will see a grey Castle at the top. It isn't as big or as fine as the Palace, but it is linked to the Well. The story is that long ago Merlin visited the Island. He liked it so much he built this Castle to stay in, and before he left he built the Well as a thankyou gift to the islanders. He blessed the stream and told the Meridos that if they throw a pebble into the stream and make a wish it will come true."

"Wow!" cried Sonny. "That's really interesting. Can we go inside the castle?"

"It belongs to the Sisko family. You can go in but you have to knock on the gate-keeper's door and ask to see round. He will probably ask someone to take you." Gogo asked,

"Are there any other interesting places to see in that area?" The girl took out her note-pad.

"I'll draw a little map," she said. "You take this route out of town and follow the road to Hermit's Hill. The road is a bit steep but not too bad. The Well is on the left at the end of a little path leading off the road about half-way up the hill. It is sign-posted. Travelling by trap it is about ten minutes further up to the Castle."

"Thanks!" said Gogo. "This is really helpful. Who is living in the Castle at the moment?"

"Lord Sisko," said the girl. "It's been the Sisko family home for centuries. The present Lord Sisko is the last of the line."

"The last?" queried Gogo. "You mean he isn't married?"

"No," said the girl, "though a few girls would be willing! He has a cousin who is married with two children and settled on another island so he has family, but no-one here."

"Are we likely to bump into him?" asked Sonny hopefully.

"You might. He's a keen gardener and spends a lot of his time working outside with his gardener. They produce a lot of fruit and vegetables which are brought down to our weekly market in the town square. Otherwise if Lord Sisko is indoors it will be more difficult. You would have to produce a good reason for wishing to meet him to the guard at the gate. He is royalty."

"Well thankyou a lot," said Gogo. "We'll call in here on our way back if we can to tell you what happened!" The girl smiled and wished them luck.

"This is really good," said Sonny as they climbed into the trap. "I thought we would end up wandering around aimlessly looking for hiding-places or guilty-looking islanders."

"I know! At least we've got somewhere to go, and hopefully someone to meet," said Gogo.

The two boys enjoyed the ride up the hillside. They had given the pony a drink of water, and had a bag of seed to give him at lunch-time. The views were magnificent across the mountains, and the sun was shining.

As predicted, they arrived at the Well around an hour later. A notice pointed the way along a little path to the Well.

"Did you know about King Arthur?" asked Gogo.

"Oh yes. He was a great King of England many centuries ago. So many stories and poems are written about him and his Knights that they are famous in English literature. Merlin was a seer or a wizard, and mentor to King Arthur."

"So they really existed," said Gogo.

"In Camelot yes," said Sonny. "All of the stories won't be true, but they sat round a famous Round Table for meetings, and they had ideals about bravoury and honour and chivalry. They called themselves the Knights of the Round Table."

"And the people of Meridoland think that Merlin and one of the Knights somehow visited here," said Gogo. "It's very romantic."

"Well they do seem to know a lot about him," said Sonny. "I wouldn't deny it."

"And they crossed dimensions in their dreams?" said Gogo doubtfully.

"I know. Weird. But there you are. I am no-one to challenge theories about dimensional travel am I?" said Sonny. "In any case that isn't our problem. Our problem is the ring. There is a connection between Merlin and the ring, so let's go and look at his Well."

They didn't have far to walk down the path before they came upon it under an over-hanging rock. A cave had been hollowed out into the side of the hill and you could walk all round the Well. Water dripped down through a hole in the roof of the cave into the Well.

"This is it!" said Gogo. His voice sounded hollow. They gazed down into the Well but could not see the water.

"I wonder how deep is," said Sonny. Gogo dropped a stone into it but the small splash came after a pause.

"Deep," said Gogo. "Let's make our wishes."

"No you can," said Sonny. "I'm going to keep mine in case I need it later. I might not be allowed two!"

"O.K. I'll keep mine as well so we have two wishes in case we need them," said Gogo. They returned to the trap and continued the climb to the top of the hill. By now they could see the Castle, grey, turreted and forbidding.

"Scary place to live!" said Gogo.

"Yeah. Oh look it has a moat and a draw-bridge and a port-cullis like in English castles. So that's another link with King Arthur," said Sonny.

The draw-bridge was down so they drove the pony-trap across it, under the port-cullis, and into the courtyard of the Castle.

"Everything is so still!" exclaimed Sonny, "As if no-one lives here and it is asleep waiting for someone to come and wake it up."

"You could say that," said Gogo, "or you could just say it's sinister waiting to pounce on unwary visitors."

"There's the guard. Let's ask if we can see round the Castle," said Sonny. The guard wore a red and gold tunic with black trousers and a black cap.

"Excuse me Sir," said Sonny bravely, "we wondered if you would let us look round the castle?"

"I don't know about that," said the guard, "who are you?"

"Oh sorry. This is Gogo from Pongoland and I'm Sonny, his friend. We're having two or three days' holiday in Meridoland. Someone in the town told us that this is an interesting place. We have just been to the Wishing Well."

"Alright," said the guard, "there is a boy about your age who works in the kitchen. He can take you round but there is not much to see. It is a small castle. Be careful of the walls. Some of the stone-work is a little loose, and be careful you don't slip on the stone. The steps are polished with age." He called for Danny, the boy from the kitchen. Danny was about the same height as Sonny and Gogo and was very pleased to see the two boys. To take them round the Castle was an unexpected treat.

"Do you like working here?" asked Gogo as they walked away. "I'm from Pongoland and we don't have children working there except as training."

"We don't either but my mother is the cook here, so she often brings me along in the school holidays. I love it up here. I don't mind helping out cleaning the silver and bronze. I get a new suit of clothes in return," he grinned. "My Dad works on the Castle farm down in the valley. I want to be a farmer when I grow up. Shall I take your pony?" They unfastened the pony from the cart and Danny tethered him in the courtyard.

"We've got his lunch here," said Gogo. "Maybe he'ld like it now." Danny took the food and poured it into a feeding-bag and attached it to the pony.

"O.K.," he said, "so let's go!"

"Where is Lord Sisko?" asked Gogo anxiously, "I hope he won't mind?"

"Lord Sisko?" said Danny, "No he's in the garden outside the wall. He won't mind. I often do little jobs for him. He's like my friend even."

That's like us and the King of Pongoland, thought Sonny.

"Does he live here alone?" he asked.

"Yes, by himself," Said Danny. "It's a bit lonely really."

"It must be," said Sonny, "how come he isn't married?" Might as well take the bull by the horns, he thought.

"Oh he wanted to marry Princess Ahoosti," said Danny cheerfully, "but she chose Lord Lannet."

"That was sad," said Gogo.

"Yes they all grew up together and played together, they and a few others in the town. There's a lady, Maria, who loves him, but he won't look at her. She's a teacher in the school now."

"How do you know she loves Lord Sisko?" asked Sonny, amazed that poor Lord Sisko's love-life seemed to be so well known.

"Because of them all playing together. All our parents knew Maria wanted him, but he was determined to marry Ahoosti.

"Goodness," said Gogo, "we don't know all those things about our Royal Family."

"Your Royal Family doesn't have children. It's the children who get to know these things. Ahoosti and Lannet used to be in and out of peoples' houses like Lord Sisko and Maria and others. I can remember them."

"So does Lord Sisko hate them now?" asked Gogo helpfully.

"No he doesn't hate them, but he doesn't go to the Palace," said Danny.

"Not ever?" asked Sonny.

"That is to say he doesn't go often. Sometimes he does diplomatic jobs for the King, so then he goes to discuss business, but he doesn't attend their parties, and he didn't go to the marriage."

"Well he wouldn't would he?" said Gogo.

"No but he was more fed-up than heart-broken," said Danny. "I know because he talks to me. See, be careful going up these steps. Some of the stones are a bit loose."

They had reached the bottom of a spiral staircase leading up a large tower. It was pretty dark inside, though there were a few turret windows.

"Why was he so dead-keen to marry her then?" asked Sonny.

"Oh because of King Arthur," said Danny a bit impatiently

"What?" cried Sonny, and Gogo stopped climbing.

"You mean the King who had the Round Table?" he asked.

"That's the one. Ancient history."

"But why would King Arthur have wanted Sisko to marry Ahoosti?" asked Sonny. Things were definitely weird!

"Sisko was a lonely kid in this old Castle, so he made up stories about himself. People believe Merlin built it and lived here a while, and some believe, anyway Lord Sisko believes, that King Arthur lived here too. In Lord Sisko's imagination King Arthur had a son here by some girl in the village. Lord Sisko studies all these old manuscripts in the Castle library."

"Has he got manuscripts to prove King Arthur lived here?" asked Sonny.

"Listen, the manuscripts aren't *that* old! The oldest is probably no more than five hundred years old. He thinks, or I should say he likes to pretend to think, that they record true history handed down by tradition. He says the records imply that King Arthur was here, but I've seen them. The stories about Merlin and King Arthur are long poems. That means someone made them up but Lord Sisko thinks of them as his history. He has set them to music."

"Oh dear," said Sonny sadly.

"Oh yes," said Danny, "he's got this big idea that he is a descendent of King Arthur. His family has always lived in this Castle you see. I don't try to contradict him, but Merlin was here well over a thousand years ago. I do believe that. This is a seriously strange place. But King Arthur? And a son in Meridoland? No evidence I say. Lord Sisko's problem was being alone here so much as a child, and you know how you imagine things when you are a child. His parents were always busy, and away a lot. No-one to put him straight, and they died before he was grown up."

"It's really sad, isn't it?" said Sonny.

"Yes it is. He tells me because I am a child. He trusts me to take him seriously. He knows, I suppose, no grown-up would. I have been like his playmate sometimes. Not so much now. After playing in the village the other kids went home, but he had to come back here."

"I expect he had to tell himself stories to stop himself from being frightened!" said Sonny. "Does Maria know about his stories?"

"Don't know," said Danny. "He doesn't talk about her. See, this is Lord Sisko's room. We can just peep in." Danny pushed open a heavy wooden door with a large iron ring on it. Inside the room was unexpectedly cheerful! The bed had a colourful patchwork quilt. A fire was laid before a thick red woollen rug. There were gleaming brass fire-irons in the hearth. On the mantle-piece were ornaments and pictures. There was a large book-case with interesting-looking books.

"Very nice!" exclaimed Sonny.

"Yes it is," said Danny. "His Mum set it up for him originally. Come along. I'll show you the library." He closed the door, and they went along the corridor to the next room. This too had a heavy door, very old. The room smelt of old parchment. There was no fire-place but there was a long table with four chairs drawn up to it.

"Come in." said Danny. "He won't mind if I show you the books. These aren't the ordinary readable books," he joked. "This is stuff for scholars, but after all he is a scholar.

"Oh, he's a scholar? So why does he believe in the poems?" asked Sonny.

"Because he wants to," said Danny. "His father never thought he was descended from King Arthur, though he once said he thought the King might be."

"The King of Meridoland descended from King Arthur?" cried Gogo. "That is as fantastic an idea as Lord Sisko being a descendent!"

"Yes it probably is," said Danny, "but look under the surface here and you do find these theories going around. I don't think the King himself thinks so, but that Merlin built the Castle? That is a general belief. And gave us the Well? You bet!"

"Well I think it's awful that Lord Sisko should spend his life here alone because he thinks he should have married Princess Ahoosti, and why? Because he thinks he's descended from King Arthur?" exclaimed Sonny.

"Therefore," pointed out Danny, "he should be next King of Meridoland."

"Oh!!" cried Sonny. "Right!!"

"Yes," said Danny. "His rightful heritage."

There was silence for a moment while Sonny and Gogo digested this bombshell.

"O.K.," said Gogo, "but he didn't marry her. Can't he just get over it and marry someone else?"

"He's fixated," said Danny. "You can't talk sense into him. I've tried."

"Wow," said Sonny, "what a conundrum! Er....you know this ring which the King has lost? That was supposed to have been given to his ancestor by Merlin for slaying a dragon. Do you think that is true?"

"Yes," said Danny. "We believe that. The ring is there after all, and there are records in the Palace of the amazing feats and achievements of all the Kings and Queens."

"Do you have any theories about where the ring went?" asked Gogo. "They have scoured the Palace for the ring."

"No idea," said Danny briefly. Sonny looked at Gogo.

"What properties does it have?" asked Sonny.

"How would I know?" asked Danny. "No-one talks about that. The King just wears it as a memorial. That's all."

"No. I just wondered. If Merlin gave it to the King at that time, don't you think he might have blessed it, as he did the Well, so that each King would receive his blessing?"

Danny stared at him.

"I never thought of that," he said.

"He very well might have Danny. Think about it," said Sonny. "Merlin wouldn't just have said, 'here, take this ring as a keepsake,' would he? These were royal people. There would have been a ceremony, a sacred ceremony, and you can bet anything the ring was blessed, like even wedding-rings are blessed, but if Merlin blesses a thing it jolly well stays blessed!"

"Gosh yes," he breathed.

It's now or never, thought Sonny.

"Danny, has Lord Sisko been to the Palace recently at all?" Danny stared at Sonny.

"You mean.........?"

"Yes, and just think of that also. He's alone here in the Castle, fixated on King Arthur, and how he has lost his chances. What might he do?"

"I'd have to look in his room," said Danny.

"Well would you mind very much just doing that right now please?" asked Sonny. "Meanwhile Gogo and I will search the library."

"Alright, but only if you promise faithfully you will never tell anybody?" said Danny.

"We promise," said Sonny. "It will just be between the three of us. Right Gogo?"

"Agreed," said Gogo.

Danny went back to Lord Sisko's bedroom while Sonny and Gogo studied the walls and books of the library.

"It need not be such a very secret place, after all," reasoned Sonny. "There's only Danny and his Mum work in the Castle from what I can see. They won't be poking around."

"True," said Gogo, "we need some little compartment, or box, or behind some special book?"

"Book!" cried Sonny. "King Arthur?"

They searched the shelves of ancient history. There was a brown leather-covered tome called simply 'Merlin'. Sonny stood on a chair and lifted it down. He opened the front cover, and discovered, rather to his horror until he realized it wasn't a real book, that a hole had been carved out of the blank pages, and in the hole lay a gold ring with a splendid dragon inlaid in it in ruby and amber and quartz.

"Gogo....." he whispered.

Quickley he lifted out the ring, closed and replaced the book, and climbed down from the chair. They examined the ring and marveled at its' workmanship. However there was no time to lose. Gogo put the chair back in its' place and they left the library, closing the door carefully behind them. They met Danny in the corridor, returning from Lord Sisko's bedroom.

"Nothing there," he reported. "What have you got there?" They showed him the ring.

"Oh no!" he cried. "Sisko *stole* it!"

"No," said Sonny firmly. "He borrowed it. He wanted to commune with it somehow and feel close to Merlin. He's been in great distress. He was looking for help."

"You are very nice boys," said Danny. "You'ld better just take it as fast as possible back to the Palace. But you won't tell where you found it, like you promised?"

"We won't," said Gogo. "The main thing is we have found it, and Meridoland will feel at peace again."

They hurried down the steps and climbed into the pony-trap. The pony had finished his food and was ready to go. Danny stood by the trap looking up at them.

"I hope I see you both again," he said, "don't forget me."

"Never," said Gogo, "when all this is over we'll come again to say thankyou."

"What happened here?" asked Sonny. "What made Lord Sisko do this now?"

"Oh! That's easy I think," said Danny. "Princess Ahoosti is expecting a baby. He may have thought it's now or never to make his claim. Desperation really," he added sadly.

"Someone saw a light in the sky," said Sonny. "Might that have been Merlin?"

"Who knows?" said Danny. "Maybe someone will write a song about that one day."

"What *you* need to do," said Sonny to Danny very firmly, "is get Sisko and Maria together. Use your imagination! Do something! Merlin *might* have come in response to a cry from Lord Sisko you know! Who else is there but you to help?" Danny laughed.

"You have given me a mission! I will do my best" he promised.

When Sonny and Gogo returned to the Palace with the ring that evening the King couldn't believe his eyes!

"I'm stunned!" he cried. "Where was it?"

"We are pledged to secrecy," said Gogo. "But Sir, would you mind if we return to Pongoland right away? This has been a wonderful visit. We have really enjoyed ourselves, but I do feel we shouldn't linger."

Goggles was waiting in the courtyard to hear about their progress, so a Palace servant went up to Sonny and Gogo's bedroom to fetch their luggage.

"I hope there aren't going to be any repercussions," said the King doubtfully.

"Whatever might be said, you know nothing about anything," said Gogo. "You can make up a cover story about how the ring was returned if you like. We can guarantee no-one will argue."

"Alright, well many many thanks boys. I do hope one day I can repay you."

With that Sonny and Gogo climbed on to Goggles' back, and in no time away they were flying home.

When they arrived back in Pongoland everything seemed to be as usual. Goggles took the boys straight to Gogo's house. Tobo rushed out, overjoyed to see them.

"What happened? Did you find it?" he asked excitedly. His parents were on his heels equally happy, if anxious, to see them.

"Yes!" said Gogo. "Mission accomplished!"

They went indoors, and sat down to a sumptuous tea of salad, fruit trifle, scones, and a sponge cake. Never was such a joyful celebration!

"And you can never tell us where you found it?" said Murgo later.

"That's right. We promised, but we placed the ring back in the hand of the King, so that was all that mattered," said Sonny.

"And all's well that ends well," smiled Gogo.

Chapter Four

The Tower of Tolikland

The King of Pongoland was delighted with the results of the ring of the Dragon's Hair test. Although he had talked to Sonny and Gogo, and they had told him what they could, he had had to allow them their secret as to where they had found it.

"Ah well," he said, "a lot of work among the Islands involves diplomacy, so in this case I have to respect your secret. But very well done, and thankyou boys."

That was all Sonny and Gogo needed. The King's approval was always sufficient reward. He said they needed a rest before their next test, so for some weeks there was no talk of expeditions. The King, however, asked Sonny to stay at the Palace one night a month. He said Sonny must become familiar with the ways of the Palace. He needed to learn who was who, and how each of the Palace staff was to be treated. Each had an individual role, and each needed understanding of his role.

In addition the King had appointed a tutor to teach Sonny the history of the Islands, as well as the geography of the whole archipelago. He needed to learn about the people and the customs of each Island, and about Pongo relations with the different Islands. So during his stay at the Palace he had an hour of history and an hour of geography. Sonny's parents agreed that one Saturday night a month he would sleep at the Pongo Palace. That meant Saturday and Saturday night in this world's terms. He returned home by evening, and went to bed late.

Otherwise he spent time in Gogo's home with Gogo talking to Murgo about his work. They both spent time in the mills and the mines, and visiting the farms on the Island. They talked with the adults, learning about their work and their problems, and they were shown how things were done. They played too in the meadow and practised their athletic skills. Sonny, Gogo, and Tobo all planned to compete in the next Sports Day.

After a few weeks the King invited Sonny and Gogo tp come to the Palace to learn about their next test. This was in connection with the mystery of the Tolik tower.

"It is the most amazing thing, boys," said the King. "The owls, and people who have been to Tolikland in recent weeks, describe this tall narrow tower reaching to the sky, and built of some sort of shiny reflecting material. It seems to be black. The Toliks refuse to say a word about it. You know that of the Islands Tolikland does have a reputation, not of criminal activities of course, but sometimes of suspicious activities that make others worry about what is going on. Odd things you know. Everything they do is not always in the best interests of the Islands as a community. So this secrecy is a matter of concern."

"So you would like us to go and find out what it is and what it is for," said Sonny.

"Precisely," said the King, "and that's not going to be easy because if they've got a secret you won't be welcome! And it won't be easy forcing your presence around the Island if they don't want you!"

"Oh dear," said Gogo, "it's going to be really awkward!"

"Yes it is," said the King, "and that is the test. To insinuate yourselves into their confidence, or at least into the Island for a stay in the first place, and then to find out what they have built. I am most eager to know!"

Tolikland was quite a long distance away from Pongoland, but could be reached by making a stop-over in Galipoland. The Galips were friends of the Pongos once the business of a certain incident with Mother Fulati had been sorted out, and Sonny and Gogo were able to get refreshments for themselves and Goggles. They allowed Goggles an hour's rest before setting off again on the second leg of their journey.

The boys weren't greatly keen to see the Island. Their only experience with Toliks had been when a Tolik man had come to stay in Pongoland in order supposedly to learn metal-work. It turned out that he had not wanted to learn how to craft gold and silver into beautiful objects, but had come to steal a large quantity. Two other Toliks had arrived to help carry the stuff away. Unfortunately for them Murgo had arranged a family picnic near the spot where the two arrived, and they had been seen. Sonny and Gogo had sat on their birds to prevent them from escaping with their loot. Murgo had called the Palace guards to arrest the Toliks.

As a result Sonny and Gogo were not feeling too friendly as they approached the Island. All the same the dominating feature of the landscape was this very tall, narrow, black tower, and they were amazed!

"What can it be?" exclaimed Gogo.

"It doesn't look like anything except a tall square pole made of something like black glass or steel," said Sonny.

"How tall would you say? Fifty feet?"

"Don't know but this is certainly an interesting investigation," said Sonny.

Goggles landed on some spare land around the pole, and they got off his back to go and take a closer look at the object. A Tolik man was sitting close by it and looked at them suspiciuously.

"Where have you come from? Pongoland?" he asked.

"That's right," said Gogo, "what's this?"

"Have you come all the way from Pongoland just to ask that?" said the man, looking gratified.

"Not entirely," said Sonny vaguely. "Is it yours?"

The man stood up. Toliks were mostly quite tall and thin with brown hair.

"No," he said. "I'm protecting it. I'm on guard."

"Protecting it from whom?" asked Gogo.

"Anybody. It's precious."

"Is it a work of art?" guessed Sonny.

"You could call it that," said the man.

"Or a watch-tower? Does it have a periscope mirror at the top?"

"No," said the man, enjoying himself now, "it's not a watch-tower, though I expect we could attach a mirror at the top if we wanted."

"Who's 'we'," asked Sonny.

"The King and his staff," said the man.

"Right," said Sonny, "so the King built it?"

"And his staff," said the man.

"What for?" asked Gogo.

"For his own purposes. Wouldn't you like a drink or something?" Clearly the man was flustered now by all the questions.

"Is there anywhere we can stay overnight?" asked Gogo. "Pongoland is too far away to come and return in one day."

"I don't know. I'll have to ask," said the man, "but we've got a tent here with refreshments for the guards. We take shifts. Come along. You can have something to drink, and your owl would like water I expect."

Sonny and Gogo were relieved to find the man quite friendly really. It seemed the Toliks weren't all hostile!

"Thankyou," said Sonny, "that would be really nice."

"You aren't a Pongo," remarked the Tolik.

"No, I'm a friend of Gogo here, and visit quite often. I live somewhere else mostly."

The man led them to a little blue and white tent erected in the shadow of some cliffs. Little seats and tables were arranged outside, and a Tolik girl came out with a tray. She had automatically poured out juice for three. She went back and brought out a bowl of water for Goggles. This was all very hospitable and not at all what Sonny and Gogo had expected.

"How long will you be here guarding the pole," asked Gogo.

"Tower," said the man. "Oh for quite some time. A lot of people want to see it. We have set up this tent partly so visitors can sit and look at it."

Sonny and Gogo looked dubious.

"I'm Sonny," he said, "and this is Gogo."

"I am Flinn and this is Bella," replied Flinn.

"So the tower is like...entertainment?" asked Gogo.

"You might call it that," said Flinn.

"In that case," said Sonny, "you need more things for people to look at when they get here. One narrow tower isn't enough."

"Lots of people love it," said Flinn defensively, "you'd be surprised how many people we serve in this tent every day."

"So it is a sight for people to come and see," said Sonny.

"You could call it that too," said Flinn.

"But Flinn!" cried Sonny, "you need to develop this place!"

"It doesn't need anything," said Flinn firmly, "it's beautiful as it is. You can see it for miles as you approach on a bird."

"That's true," said Gogo.

"Yes....well......no-one thinks the Toliks can do anything. Then when we do everybody criticizes," grumbled Flinn.

"Who's 'everybody'?" asked Sonny.

"Well you two, and a few others who have been from other Islands. We in Tolikland like it just as it is."

He retired to sit by the tower in a huff.

"Right," said Sonny to Gogo, "it's meant to be a tourist attraction."

"Wow," said Gogo, "you'd have to be seriously bored to come and look at it."

"Well we've come," said Sonny.

"Yes because the King wanted to know what the Toliks were up to! We wouldn't travel a day to see a possible work of art, but probably not."

"No," said Sonny, "still I feel sorry for Flinn. He seems proud of it."

Gogo went over to the table where Bella was arranging plates of sandwiches and buns.

"Hello Bella, is the tower all you've got to show us, or is there anything else around here?"

Bella turned pink, ashamed or embarrassed.

"You shouldn't have made Flinn feel small," she said.

"Feel small?" exclaimed Gogo. "We were just asking what it was."

Well he designed it, and he's very proud of it, and you didn't praise it," said Bella. "That sort of thing makes people feel small."

"Oh sorry," said Gogo.

"Who asked him to design it?" asked Sonny, coming up.

"The King asked for designs for a spectacular attraction," said Bella.

"OK so Flinn certainly succeeded," admitted Sonny. "What did he get? A prize?"

"Yes he did," said Bella defensively.

"What else was produced?" asked Gogo. "Everything ought to be on display here, and that would make an exhibition of Tolik handicrafts."

"I don't know," said Bella."The King just put the tower up and this tent." She offered sandwiches and buns to the boys, so they went back to their table to eat."

"Something's wrong, isn't it?" said Gogo when they were alone.

"Yeah," said Sonny. "Weird I'ld say. Something is certainly wrong here."

"Looks as if people have nothing to do and nowhere to go, if this place is typical of Tolikland."

"That Tolik who came to Pongoland to learn metal-craft?" said Sonny. "The King had sent him, hadn't he? He wasn't supposed to steal. He was supposed to get some training. The Tolik King was very angry about the robbery wasn't he?"

"He certainly was," said Gogo. "He was livid. He'ld had some idea of building up an industry here."

"You know, we sort of represent our King here," said Sonny. "Not exactly, but he sent us. I think we should go to the Tolik Palace and see if we can find out what's going on. I wonder if the Palace is far from here."

"Good idea, but what shall we say we've come about?"

"We could start with mentioning that thief – what was his name?"

"Kilti."

"Kilti, and that as we were in Tolikland we thought we'ld ask how he's doing," said Sonny.

"Is the King going to want to be reminded about him? It's hardly tactful to mention him."

"O.K. maybe not," said Sonny, "But why are we here? Unless we blow up all this stuff about the tower. Say our King had heard about it and wanted us to see it etc etc? So we wanted to ask about the idea behind it."

"Alright. We'll just have to fudge it along. I'll ask Bella the way to the Palace," said Gogo.

It seemed the distance to the Palace was walkable so they left Goggles to eat and relax, and set off along the road Bella had pointed to. The Tolik scenery was really very attractive with cliffs, and hills covered with thick woodland, and a valley through which a river ran southwards to somewhere. Was there sea on this Island, Sonny wondered. But where would the edge be?

The Palace stood on a rocky promontory, overlooking the river. A path and then steps led up to a high wooden gate.

"More adventures!" whispered Gogo.

"Yes, this is a bit nerve-wracking though. I wonder what the King is like," said Sonny.

There was a long bell-rope, so they pulled it and heard a distant gong. Then a shuffling of feet, and the door was opened by an elderly man in a maroon uniform with a cap. He was very surprised to see two boys, but Gogo told him they had come from the King of Pongoland, so they were invited in. They entered a cobbled court-yard with trees overhanging it, and in the centre there was a little well with a seat all round it. They walked past this and into the Palace itself. The boys found themselves in a large hall with a tiled floor. Above it was a very high glassed dome. Around the walls the boys saw old paintings of bygone Tolik monarchs and their families.

"It's a bit fusty isn't it?" whispered Sonny.

"Yeah. A bit sort of dead," said Gogo. "Everything still."

In a few minutes the man returned to take them to the King. They were invited into a large sitting-room, furnished comfortably, if a little shabbily, with sofas and arm-chairs. The King and Queen were seated in front of a high fire-place. The King was dressed informally in a dark green tunic with black trousers, and the Queen wore a sprigged muslin full-length dress. They asked the boys to join them by the fire.

"Well, this is a surprise," said the King. "Have you travelled all this way by yourselves from Pongoland to see me?"

"Our King was very intrigued, Sir, to hear about your amazing new sculpture," said Sonny. "A lot of people have been talking about it, and he wanted to learn more about how it looks and who made it."

You can't get more diplomatic than that, thought Sonny. He caught an admiring glance from Gogo. However the King was not fooled.

"Come, come, young man," said the King, "you can't flannel me. That pole is bizarre!" Sonny and Gogo were stunned.

"Tower," corrected Gogo inadvertently.

"Oh! You've been talking to Flinn? Tower then."

"Don't you like it?" asked Sonny incredulous. "You awarded him a prize."

"I had offered a prize, and his was the only contribution, so he got the prize, that's all. Be honest. What did you feel when you saw it?"

The boys shifted uneasily. This was so embarrassing.

"Curiosity!" Sonny came up with.

"Bravo," said the King, "a quick wit! And when you looked closer?"

"Er, we asked Flinn if it was a work of art, or just a sight to come and look at, or maybe an entertainment," said Gogo. "But he wouldn't commit himself."

"That's because he just built a tower of bricks essentially, slightly expensive ones but that's all they are, and he had to borrow a step-ladder from the Palace. The pole goes up as high as our tallest step-ladder."

Gogo burst out laughing. Sonny looked scandalized at his friend's lapse, but he had set the King and Queen off laughing too. The Queen rang for someone to bring refreshments.

"OK," said the King. "Now I have come clean, I pray you will. You did not travel all this way to look at Flinn's pole!"

"We did Sir, truly," said Sonny, "but that was because our King was worried about it."

"He wondered what we were up to," said the King.

"Something like that," said Sonny. "Well not that quite, but he was curious."

"Yes I see," said the King. "After that attempted theft by Kilti we were deeply mortified. Tolikland has been declining for some years. We do wood-carvings, but no-one wants wooden utensils nowadays. Galipoland produces all that wonderful crockery. We have learnt that we can't compete equally amongst the Islands and have nothing to produce for the Trade Fair. You have to take enough of your own produce to have something to exchange for other peoples'. We survive here mostly on our own produce. We have become self-subsisting, but our people have grown lethargic. They are bored. I had thought we might buy raw materials from other Islands to make utensils and household items ourselves, so I sent Kilti to learn some skills, but he let us down so badly we could hardly hold our heads up after that. We didn't even attend the last Trade Fair."

"I think you aren't the only Island which has had that problem in competing in a market which is dominated by those who have a lot to offer," said Sonny, remembering another Island which had had a similar problem but which had turned itself around with a bit of initiative and a lot of hard work.

"So you were trying to stimulate some talent when you announced the competition?"

"Exactly right," said the King. "I thought Tolikland can't be entirely without talent. It's just that those who have it haven't been motivated to use it. However, only Flinn responded," he sighed. The Queen shook her head.

"I wanted to get our women into weaving or knitting, but we would have to buy the wool from somewhere." Sonny couldn't believe what he was hearing. All this was pretty pathetic. Those Islands did well where the King and Queen were energetic about organizing production and trade. Things didn't happen without effort. This Island had a surplus of wood, and a big potential for sheep-rearing, just for starters. So OK, plunge in.

"Yes, I see your problem but shouldn't someone be managing your land? If you had a lot of sheep you would have plenty of wool. You could have distinctive Tolik rugs, say, with a local design. If that pole got famous as a local landmark it could even feature as your Tolik trademark for woolen goods! I mean I'm just playing with ideas. Tolik sweaters. You have a lot of wood. You could make ladders, wooden buckets, furnishings. The list is endless."

So why don't you? He thought. The King sighed.

"You make it sound so simple," he said glumly.

"Pongoland has farm-land maintained for sheep and goats, extensive woodland which provides ingredients for Mother Fulati's medicines, and lowland where sheds are built for spinning and weving. The rocky areas are mined for precious minerals, and a lot of the men of the Island sit all day fashioning beautiful things. Everybody works, Sir," said Sonny.

"We seem to have sunk into depression, I suppose," sighed the King. "We think beforehand that we will fail, whatever we do."

"Why not let your young people get busy on something?" suggested Gogo. "Our King had an athletics field set up, and built a swimming-pool, and all the young people train to take part in an Annual Sports Day. The young people of Meridoland are very musical and produce wonderful concerts!"

"Yes all that sounds wonderful," grumbled the King, "but look what happened when I organized a talent contest! I got one tower of bricks."

Sonny and Gogo smiled.

"Well we come from a very energetic Island," said Gogo. "How would it be if we were to wander round Tolikland a bit talking to people, and possibly ferreting out latent ambitions?"

The King waved a hand.

"Do, do," he said, "find all the latent ambition you can! I'll be delighted. But you will discover this is a dull-as-lead Island. Nothing happens."

"Well I've got one idea," said Sonny, "if you don't mind me making suggestions here and there."

"Not at all! Not at all!" said the King who seemed too lethargic even to ask what the idea was. No leadership, thought Sonny. Hopeless. The Queen roused herself to say they must stay at the Palace while they were in Tolikland. She was a kindly woman, and told them to go and come as they wished. Dinner would be at eight, and they would have a room in the Palace.

So that was that sorted, thought Gogo. The boys excused themselves and left the Palace.

"Wow!" said Gogo, "compare them with our King and Queen!"

"I know," said Sonny. "We're going to have to work very hard during our time here if we are going to get anything started. Even Flinn is just sitting by his tower. What's the matter with them all?"

"Well Bella was walking backwards and forwards, and preparing food," said Gogo.

"True. My first idea was for that land by the tower. They could make an amusement park there. I can see it all!" said Sonny, his eyes sparkling. "They could attach a big wheel to the tower. A little restaurant can be built where the tent is. There can be swings and roundabouts and a Big Dipper. Games. And what do you need to build those things? Wood! We need some musical people to create music there. Just imagine Gogo! A first class amusement park right there where the birds from other Islands land! You could have people arriving in droves with their children for a day out in Tolikland! Good food, skittles, a bowling ally, a shooting range!"

"I can see why the King wants you to succeed him," smiled Gogo. "Some of those things you mention though might not be known in the Islands. You would have to explain them."

"Of course. Glad to help. I can see it all!" he repeated, "Let's go and wake up Tolikland."

"Sonny," said Gogo anxiously, "how would people pay for their turns on the roundabouts and everything?" He had been around enough in Sonny's world to have seen fair-grounds, and knew that there you needed money!

"We'll think about in detail that later. People would have to bring goods from their own Island, and a Tolik could assess the worth. Or better, there could be some sort of catalogue containing lists of items for exchange in return for so many hours in the park. Something like that. Perishables would have to be used by the Toliks, or in the restaurant, but other stuff could be stored to take to the Trade Fair."

Gogo began to feel excited too, but implementing the ideas was another thing.

"We'd better talk to Bella then. Flinn won't be able to help. Bella was working her socks off, a bit fed up maybe, but not defeated."

"You're right," said Sonny. "Let's start with Bella."

As they walked back to the tower Sonny added,

"What I feel is if we can get them enthusiastic about the amusement park idea and using their wood to make the equipment, carpenters would have to be properly trained for the work and then hopefully persuaded to go on and make other things. There must be carpenters here, so they could train others. Then you'll have them producing things to barter."

"Sometimes I forget we're children," said Gogo.

"We have to forget that if we are going to stir people up!" said Sonny.

When they arrived back at the tent Bella was sitting having a cup of tea herself. With her was another girl.

"Hello," she said, "this is my friend Tania. I've been telling her about your visit."

"Yes," said Tania. "You think that tower is pretty tacky huh?"

"Er……well……..," mumbled Sonny.

"No. Be frank," said Tania.

"The thing is, I think it's got potential," said Sonny. Bella's ears pricked up.

"Oh do you? Flinn is so depressed. No-one is really coming to view his work. A few drop by for a cup of tea."

"The thing is that by itself it isn't enough to attract crowds," said Gogo. Tania collapsed in giggles. Bella ignored her.

"So what do you think we can do to improve things?"

"Build an Amusement Park," said Sonny firmly. No time to beat about the bush.

"A…a…what?" asked Tania.

"You know…….swings, roundabouts, slide, games, toffee apples, candy floss, the lot!"

"So, where does Flinn's tower fit into it?" asked Tania. Sonny was encouraged that the girls didn't just laugh at him. Instead they were trying to visualize what he was describing.

"That will be really useful," said Sonny to Bella. "We can attach the Big Wheel to it. Of course it will need supports."

"Right," said Bella. "Wow. Who's going to do all that though? You will have noticed how things are here."

"Well there are you two, and we will help. Don't you have friends who would love to get involved in doing something really exciting? We'll need a lot of wood and trained carpenters. You must have them?"

"Yes of course. Who do you think makes all our stuff?" said Tania.

"So could we present our ideas to them, and ask them to take charge of building the equipment? Gogo and I will draw sketches showing what we need. And we will need stalls for games and snacks."

"Do you have anyone who is musical?" asked Gogo. "You can't have an amusement park without lots of music!"

"Yes.........," said Bella doubtfully, "we do but they are very angry."

"How so?" asked Sonny. Bella sighed.

"They'll be in the village hall now. There is a good musical group. They call themselves Dark Danger and they are led by the King's son Prince Carlos."

"Heavens!!' exclaimed Sonny. "The King and Queen never mentioned him!"

"No well, there's bad feeling!" said Bella.

"Prince Carlos is one of the angry young people?" said Gogo.

"You bet!"

"May we come and meet them now?" asked Sonny. "We don't have too much time really. Everyone will get worried in Pongoland if we delay much."

Bella and Tania led the boys to their pony-trap. The pony had been grazing and lifted its' head expectantly as they approached. He was hitched on to the trap and they all climbed in. It was a short ride to Tolikland's main town centre. There was a central social area with seats and lawn and trees, and round the perimeter of the square there were shops, some houses, and a large building which turned out to be the Community Hall. It was painted white and had a red tiled roof. Bella drove the trap round and came to a halt in front of it. They all climbed down from the trap and on Bella's bidding, climbed the three steps up to the main entrance. The building had tall windows and two large doors.

Inside there was a big hall. The atmosphere was rather dusty, and there was a good deal of noise. At the opposite end to the door there was a low stage, and several young people were practising on their musical instruments. About a couple of dozen other young people thronged the hall shouting to each other and laughing. Someone threw a ball. As the four of them entered the room they all fell quiet, deeply curious and maybe apprehensive. A boy called,

"Hello Bella! Hello Tania!"

"Hi Bailey!" Bella called back. She led Sonny and Gogo down the hall to introduce them.

"These are Sonny and Gogo from Pongoland. They are visiting. They thought Tolikland seemed a bit dull I think, so I brought them here. They wanted to know if we have any music." She turned to Sonny and Gogo. "These are Dark Danger, our scary music group!" she laughed.

A dark-haired, darker-skinned boy perched on the edge of the stage looked up. He had brown eyes, though most of the Toliks seemed to have green eyes. The Royal Families of the Islands inter-married so that their physical characteristics were often different from the Islanders' own.

"This is Prince Carlos," said Tania. "He is the leader of the group and plays the guitar. And this is Andrea," she said turning to another boy close by. "He plays the harmonica. When they are all here there are six in the group."

Prince Carlos looked watchful, as if suspicious about their intentions. Andrea was out-going and greeted them in a friendly way.

"Glad to meet you," he said. "How long are you staying?"

"Not long," said Sonny. Might as well tell them….. "Our King sent us to look at your pole and report back about it. What it looks like close up and what it's for and so on."

"Our pole?" said Carlos. "Oh you mean the tower thing. What did you think it was?"

"No-one had any idea. It has created quite a stir!" said Sonny.

"Oh well good. More than any of the rest of us can claim," said Carlos.

Have to be blunt, thought Sonny.

"What's going on? You look like a cell of revolutionaries!" he laughed. Immediately Carlos was on his feet, angry.

"What do you mean a 'cell'? Who said that?"

"It's just that you look as if something is going on. A cell means a small number of people dedicated to bringing about change, often through violence." Gogo was looking very uneasy indeed. Sonny was in way over his head here. Prince Carlos stared hard at Sonny for a few long moments.

"You are far too young to be a spy for a counter-revolution!" he remarked, relaxing. "You are very intuitive though. A revolution is indeed in the making, right here, right now."

"At least the tower is a talking-point," said Sonny, "and I've got ideas about how you can develop something really productive and interesting around it."

"So you're not only intuitive! You've got ideas! The King of Pongoland has a right to wonder what we Toliks might be up to, but sadly that tower of bricks is our only claim to fame currently. Not that you can knock it over like a toy. Its' foundation goes down three feet into the ground, and metal supports run all the way up its' four corners. Reflecting polished slates of granite form the sides, and they are glued together with builders' glue. Flinn worked very hard on it. The ladder he borrowed reaches to the roof of the inside of the Palace dome, so that's its' height." He smiled, and Sonny and Gogo suddenly saw his underlying charm.

"Hats off to Flinn, I say," said Carlos. "While others stared at their navels he worked hard, and I shall never forget it." Bella smiled, pink with pleasure, and storing up the Prince's words to tell Flinn later.

So," said Sonny, getting to his point, "we can safely attach the Big Wheel to it."

You could hear a pin drop.

"What!" said Carlos. "What big wheel? For water from the river?"

"No no no," laughed Sonny. "The Big Wheel some of us are planning for the Amusement Park on that site."

"Just a minute! Just a minute! Just four beats to the bar! What Amusement Park is who planning?" said Carlos.

62

"A few of us. That is Bella, Tania, Gogo, and me. We can draw you the plans if you have time?" said Sonny. "A Fair-Ground? The Big Wheel of course with seats on it all round, several roundabouts, big swings, a Big Dipper, slide, amusement galleries with skittles, a bowling ally, a shooting ally, coconut shies, snacks like candy-floss, toffee apples, ice-cream. AND - lots of music! That was why we wanted to come here and meet you now. Your group could be on a grandstand there, and keep everyone entertained with music. That land is where the birds arrive from other Islands, so you should have lots of visitors coming in with their children for a day out!" Prince Carlos just stared.

"And," pressed on Sonny while he had the advantage, "to build all the equipment you will need to use lots of your wood! Your carpenters can train apprentices up to be master carpenters while they work on the fair-ground. Then they will be qualified to make useful or decorative items to bring to the Trade Fair! Of course there is the issue of the exchange rate of produce people will need to bring for their day in the Amusement Park. We were thinking maybe you could draw up a catalogue listing the value in terms of hours at the Fair of common items of produce used for barter among the Islands. Something on those lines. Of course that needs hammering out, and there is the question of perishables which would have to be consumed by your Islanders, or used in the little restaurant we thought would be good to replace the tent? Balla could run that very well with Tania maybe if they liked."

"WAIT!" bellowed Carlos. "Your ideas are criss-crossing with my ideas, and you aren't even Toliks!" Sonny paused.

"Your ideas? What are you planning?"

"Like we said. A revolution, but you have to swear allegiance before I tell you anything," said Carlos.

"We can't swear allegiance to you Carlos," said Gogo. "We owe allegiance to the King of Pongoland."

"Alright then," said Carlos, "but you have to promise secrecy." Sonny met Gogo's eyes.

"We're good at that," he said.

"Alright. Everyone here is in on this. We are going to lock up the King in part of the Palace, and I'm going to take over as Prince Regent."

"Lock up your father!" exclaimed Gogo.

"You bet. He's had years to turn things around here, and what has he done? Nothing. And when I begged, implored, him to make changes in Tolikland, he announced a competition! And you've seen what that produced. No. Our patience is worn out. I shall send my mother to Rainbowland to her family, and just take over. Then you'll see what Tolikland can do."

"Can't you send your father to Rainbowland too?" asked Gogo.

"No. The birds wouldn't take him. I'll ask my mother nicely to visit her family for a few weeks, and she will go."

"So what are your plans once you are Regent?" asked Sonny eagerly.

"That's what we have been planning," said Andrea mysteriously.

"And?" asked Sonny.

"You ask too many questions. We haven't finalized those yet. First things first," said Carlos.

"You mean you haven't got any ideas either!" accused Sonny. "What you'll end up doing is take over the Palace and having big parties!"

"No!" said Andrea, annoyed. "The trouble is Tolikland has become like a lake in which all the silt has sunk to the bottom, and there isn't even a ripple. It will be difficult to work up a storm."

"Alright," said Sonny, "well call us the storm! We've got plenty of energy."

"Starting with an Amusement Park," said Andrea.

"Yes! Don't you see! That will get people stirred up. Give them each a job. Gogo and I will give you the list of the things you are going to need, and you can present it to your workmen. Gogo and I will draw sketches of the main things, but when I reach Pongoland I will send you proper pictures." (From my world, he thought.) "Get things going! Each person has to be given a responsibility. And after the Fair is built your carpenters then need to do real hard work making things for the next Trade Fair. I'll send you pictures of nice or useful things they could make. A catalogue possibly will have to be written listing all the things people are likely to bring to exchange, and you have to decide how much of each is worth how many hours in the park. You can even post lists in the landing area. Like a plain woolen shawl would mean half a day for a family till one o'clock, and an embroidered shawl would mean a whole day for a family. That sort of idea."

"Then we store up what we receive for the next Trade Fair," said Carlos.

"Yes! The Islanders are constantly exchanging goods after all," said Sonny.

"We can ask our Chief Minister to draw up the catalogue, with one of us at his elbow," said Andrea, "and send round copies to all the nearby Islands!"

"Yes. WHEN YOU ARE READY!" said Sonny firmly. "First the work has to be done. The Fair would run throughout the year, so you will need to keep adding to it to keep people interested. And Andrea you will need to work on your music. Do you have plenty of compositions?"

Andrea looked uneasy.

"OK," said Sonny. "Meridoland has wonderful musicians and a group called the Spangles. Would you like to invite them here for a week or so to work on your repertoire with you?"

"That would be really helpful," said Carlos. "We're keen you know but we may have stagnated."

"So before we leave, would you like to write a letter to the King of Meridoland asking if the Spangles might pay you a visit? I will see he gets the letter."

"Wonderful," said Carlos. "We do need some collaboration."

"You have to make friends with the other Islands. No Island survives well on its' own," said Sonny. "The Fair will help you to make lots of new friends."

"You have an old head on young shoulders, young Sonny," said Carlos.

"Other people have said that," said Gogo smiling.

"I think we need you two to stay with us a while to help us get things started," said Andrea.

"No," said Sonny. "You have to do it for yourselves. Why don't we call a meeting of the islanders tomorrow morning by the tower to discuss the whole project, and alot tasks to everyone?"

Immediately the young people in the hall were talking together excitedly, already making suggestions. Sonny took Carlos on one side.

"Why not postpone locking up your father? Have the meeting and then present the islanders' plans to him. If he still digs his feet in, then OK lock him up – temporarily, in his own rooms."

"How long are you staying?" asked Carlos.

"Three days," said Sonny.

"Counting this the first day, and leaving the day after tomorrow?"

"Yes."

"So tomorrow we hammer out a schedule for the development of the Island. Then the following day we present our ideas to my father. If he is obstructive I lock him up, comfortably of course with people to serve him. If he is interested we invite him to participate."

"That would be really good if he would. Would you like Gogo and me to prepare the way with him for you? Talk around the subject a bit. Mention the idea of an Entertainment Park centred round the tower? And possibly a carpentry industry emerging from the work entailed?"

"Yes good thinking. You seem to be pretty articulate so I'll leave that side of things to you. Don't be afraid to shake them up a bit. I shan't let Dad stop this. Tolikland is going to be as good as any other Island in the Archipelago by the time we have finished. Mother will help in her own way, I know."

That evening Sonny and Gogo didn't say anything to the King and Queen about their meeting with Carlos as it was such a difficult relationship. They went to bed early, and by nine o'clock next morning were down by the pole. They had done their best to draw images of the Big Wheel and a roundabout. Swings and slides were commonly seen in the Islands, so the helter-skelter was an easy idea. Otherwise they would send good pictures from Sonny's world, (minus people!), of the things they would need. Carlos arrived with Andrea, and three other friends, Toby, Mandy, and Minny. They studied the drawings and asked about size. Then they all studied the land and made marks where tentatively each ride might be placed.

"If you can send one of your birds with us to Pongoland I can get some proper pictures for you so that they can return with them," said

Sonny. "I'll look for things made of wood also that your carpenters might like to make for the Trade Fair."

Andrea had brought paper and pencil for them to draft out an idea of how the Amusement Park would look. Sonny showed them a traditional layout with food-stalls, games and the grandstand for a music group. He also showed them how a little restaurant could replace the blue and white tent where they could serve lunches and snacks. Carlos appointed Bella and Tania in charge of that to their huge gratification.

In due course the two carpenters arrived and Carlos showed them the sketches and the ground lay-out. He asked them to appoint three apprentices to train in carpentary, and employ them for the building of the fair-ground.

"You will also need to employ two painters," he said. "We are all going to learn now how to work really hard for our Island, and make Tolikland one of the most vibrant Islands in the Archipelago! I think you could start with the trees on the hill over-looking the Palace on the other side of the river, so go there and decide which ones to cut. You can carve them up there. We don't want a pile of saw-dust here. Then bring the planks and blocks here to build. But first we need the designs. We'll decide together what we need of what. Andrea and I will direct the construction-work so don't worry about that. Nine o'clock sharp here every morning for those not cutting wood!"

The men looked a bit dazed with this sudden rush of activity, but Carlos was well-liked and they were perfectly happy to join in his enterprise. They even felt excited, perhaps for the first time in their lives. Something was happening, and they were part of it!

"Excellent!" said Andre. "And we don't want just your work. We shall need your ideas. So get thinking!"

"One idea for the carpenters might be toys and children's games," said Tania. "They could be used as prizes, or sold, in the fair, and a lot could be stored for the Trade Fair."

"Very good ideas," said Carlos. "Keep them coming, all of you."

Sonny and Gogo felt content with the day's achievements as they returned to the Palace that evening.

"Looks quite hopeful," said Gogo.

"Yes I do hope his father isn't going to be too much of a drag."

"Well we'll do what we can to help, but in the end this is their revolution. They have to carry it through," said Gogo.

The conversation after dinner was difficult.

"We've had a few ideas for the tower," remarked Sonny.

"Oh yes? You've thought of a use for it?" asked the King.

"Yes, it could be the support for a Giant Wheel," said Sonny.

"Wh....what?"

"Yes. We met your son, Prince Carlos, and his friends in town, and they are planning to build an Amusement Park on that land," said Sonny conversationally.

"What!" cried the Queen.

"Yes Ma'am," said Sonny. "Sir," he ploughed on, "you wanted to get some activities going, and the tower won your competition. Well Carlos felt you could develop something really good around it."

"You will have heard of amusement parks and fair-grounds, Sir," said Gogo. "Swings, roundabouts, helter-skelters, that sort of thing? And you organize games like skittles and hoopla for the children, and serve refreshments. People would come a long way to spend a day in Tolikland's Amusement Park, and they would bring produce to exchange for a day's fun!"

If Carlos had wanted his parents stirred up, Sonny and Gogo had certainly done the trick!

"Anyway, if you would excuse us Sir, we have a long day ahead tomorrow, and maybe we should get to bed," said Sonny.

"Wait a minute!!" bellowed the King. "What's all this nonsense you are talking? What in the name of Tolikland is a roundapout?"

"Roundabout," corrected Gogo.

"Whatever. Who's going to build a thing like that? Who's going to manage it?"

"Your carpenters were holding a meeting today. They are getting together a team," reassured Sonny. "They are delighted with the scheme. It will bring revenue to the Island and create jobs, and they will have plenty of time left to produce useful or decorative items for the next

Trade Fair. They are quite excited. Prince Carlos is organizing everybody so probably he will manage the Amusement Park."

The King looked faint. The Queen was trying to hide a smile.

"Well done Carlos," she murmured.

"What! Not you as well!" complained her husband.

"You wanted Tolikaland to prosper dear," she said. "It rather looks as if it might! Carlos is a young man now, and perfectly capable of organizing things. He's always had plans but you always tried to squash them," she said reproachfully.

"Squash them! I know what is feasible, and what is fantasy, that's all!"

"The Amusement Park is feasible Sir," said Sonny. "He can do it. And he wants to store up merchandise to take to the Trade Fair."

"The carpenters have all sorts of ideas about what to make," said Gogo.

"When I asked for them, all their combined thought could come up with was a pole," pointed out the King.

"I know but now Prince Carlos has got them enthusiastic," said Sonny. "They are eager to help. Carlos said he would come to see you tomorrow to discuss the plans."

"Oh will he?" said the King drily.

"Yes, he wanted to get them properly thrashed out before presenting them," said Gogo.

"And if I say no?" aid the King.

"Why would you do that Sir?" asked Sonny. "You were saying yourself that the Island needs stirring up. And here is Carlos stirring! And he has loads of support, you'll see!"

"Goodnight Sir, Ma'am," said Gogo, and they softly left the room.

"Wow," breathed Sonny as they went upstairs. "That was hair-raising. We've had a lot of adventures, but I don't recall anything as scary as that."

Meanwhile Carlos had remained near the pole talking to the people of Tolikland. He told them about what he wanted for Tolikland, and how they could become great again. Everyone was to have a skill or industry. He talked about the future and how everyone's suggestions would be welcome. They were going to produce their own wool and weave it. They were going to make clothes. But they needed musicians and artists as well as farmers and craftsmen.

"So you see the sky is the limit, and each of us must think about what we will be able to contribute."

The people cheered and shouted, "Long live Carlos! Long live Carlos!"

The next morning a little delegation arrived at the Palace, to present the plans to the King. Carlos had told those closest to him what he intended to do if the King was seriously obstructive. He would be kept comfortable, but he would not be allowed to interfere with the development of Tolikland. Carlos knew in any case that his Mother would be helpful. He just felt that she might be happier with her own family for a few weeks if things turned out badly in the Palace.

Sonny and Gogo did not join them. They knew their presence would be an embarrassment.

Some time later Carlos led his delegation back down again to the crowd waiting near the pole. Prince Carlos stood on a rock to address them.

"People of Tolikland, my Father is not young now, and it is not always easy for older people to accept change. However I am here to announce that he has told me he will not stand in our way. He says history seems to be racing ahead of him, but since I seem to be at the head of the chase he feels his only choice is to let us carry out our plans for this Island. I am sure you will all want to honour his foresight and wisdom in coming to this decision, and to remember how he has served this Island faithfully all his life. He has agreed graciously to open our Entertainment Park when it is ready, and we will all want him to see what we can do!"

A great cheer went up, and shouts of,

"Long live the King! Long live the Queen! Long live Prince Carlos!"

Sonny and Gogo were watching from the back of the crowd.

"We have a lot to tell our King and Queen," murmured Gogo.

Goggles was waiting for them close by, and it was time for them to leave. They had told the Prince that they preferred to leave quietly, so they just waved as they walked to Goggles. Beside Goggles stood a Tolikland bird, ready to accompany them back in order to collect from Sonny the drawings and pictures he had promised. Carlos gave them a salute, and they grinned.

When they arrived back in Pongoland the King invited them to report to the Palace immediately, so Goggles took them to the Palace courtyard. The King and Queen were eager to hear what had happened.

"They call that pole a tower, Sir," said Gogo, "though the King just calls it a tower of bricks. It was a submission for a competition he had announced to stimulate creativity on the Island."

"That was all anyone could come up with," said Sonny. "The place was totally stagnant."

"Until you two arrived?" smiled the King.

"Well not just that," said Sonny. "Prince Carlos, who must be in his twenties, had all sorts of ideas and suggestions, but the King wouldn't listen. So we thought maybe an Amusement Park could be built on the land where the tower is."

"And that in turn would get their carpentry industry going," said Gogo. " They've got loads of woodland."

"Good thinking. But I can't wait to hear what the inert King said to that!"

"Well, Sir," said Sonny, "things are going ahead. But the rest of what happened is confidential." The King stared hard at them.

"Right," he said. "So strictly between the four of us what happened?"

"Prince Carlos was planning to lock up the King, send his Mum to Rainbowland for a while, and take over as Prince Regent."

"Oh," said the King. "Were these your suggestions?"

"Of course not!" exclaimed Sonny. "We persuaded him to cool it a bit. We described a fair-ground, and drew sketches. I have promised to send him some proper pictures which I'll get from home. One of their birds has come with us to take them back to Carlos. He's got the general idea. They've set up a little tent where people can sit and have a cup of tea while they gaze at the pole, tower that is. So where the tent is they will now build a restaurant to serve meals to all the people who come to spend a day in the fair. It's going to be great! There are two carpenters so they are going to get together a team of people who would like to learn carpentary, and they will serve their apprenticeship working on the Amusement Park. There will be games and snacks, and souvenirs to buy –"

"What with?" asked the King.

"Their Chief Minister is going to draw up a catalogue of the things people from other Islands use for barter, along with their value in terms of hours in the Amusement Park. It'll work out at half-days or full day usually to keep it simple. Then he'll send copies of the catalogue to all the neighbouring Islands. All the non-perishable stuff will be stored to take to the next Trade Fair."

"So the King is so excited about all this Carlos won't have to imprison him?"

"That's right," said Sonny. "Though of course he would just have been locked in part of the Palace with people to look after him."

"I wish I could have been a fly on the wall when Carlos broke the news," said the King.

"Oh well Gogo and I broke it," said Sonny. "Carlos wanted us to do the preparation work. Breaking the ground so he could come in the next day with the full scenario."

"Right. So what did he say?"

"He bellowed a bit and we tiptoed off to bed," said Gogo. "But the next day he accepted Carlos's plans. In any case the Queen was supportive. She pointed out to him that he had wanted Tolikland to prosper and here it was, about to prosper."

"We have brought a letter for the King of Meridoland," said Sonny. "Carlos has a musical group and he wants to invite the Spangles to pay a visit to Tolikland soon to help and advise in, I would guess, rebranding his own group. It's probably a bit fusty."

"The King and Queen of Tolikland have no idea how big a hand Sonny and I have had in the rebranding of Tolikland. That's why we need to keep what we have told you confidential, if you don't mind Sir," said Gogo.

"So the second of your great exploits must also go under the mat!" said the King. "How am I to demonstrate to Pongoland that you have proved your worth?"

"I know Sir. I can see that," said Sonny.

"Never mind. I will have to use a bit imagination myself, hinting at secrets too sensitive to divulge, whilst bolstering up what I can say to its' maximum credibility," said the King, "shaking his head. "Well let's hope the events of the third test can be blazoned forth in triumph!"

"Really I doubt it Sir," said Sonny. "We are children."

Chapter Five

The Witch of Beldeena Island

Sonny's third test did not come until into the New Year. One day in January the King invited him into his private sitting-room.

He attended classes every weekend in the Palace on the history and geography of the Islands, and on Saturday night he slept at the Palace. He was comfortable now in his little room, and had some of his own things stored away there in the cupboards, as well as his favourite books on the shelves. He was allowed to borrow whatever he liked from the Palace library, so quite a lot of his time went in reading the famous stories and legends of the Islands. From his window he could see Murgo's house, and Sonny, Gogo, and Tobo had torches to signal goodnight to each other.

When he entered the King's sitting-room on that January day the King said,

"Sonny you must have been wondering about your third test. I didn't want just to make up some test. It needed to be real. Now a real test has come along."

Sonny looked curious.

"Have you heard of Beldeena Island?"

"No Sir," said Sonny.

"Well it's a long way from here, so we hardly ever go there. Three birds and two over-night stays on the way. Anyway they have their own Wise Woman, rather like our Mother Fulati. Because of the distance the two don't meet much. It's not just that the birds get tired. The riders get tired too. However Mother Fulati has raised a matter of concern. She fears that this witch, (she calls herself a white witch), is involved in making some preparation which has noxious side-effects."

Sonny was surprised. Mother Fulati's rules were always very strict about what she made. No harm was ever done, and non had unpleasant side-effects. Some had unusual pleasant side-effects, as Sonny himself had seen, but there was a serious purpose for these, and they soon wore off.

"I don't wish to send Mother Fulati all that way, though she asked to go, because we need her here. I can't spare her. And Mother Fulati also feels that if Eleanor, (that's her name), does have a guilty secret she will immediately assume, if Mother Fulati suddenly turns up, that she has come to ferret out the secret. Naturally Eleanor would hide it."

Sonny nodded, seeing where this was going.

"What sort of noxious effects does the preparation have? What is it prescribed for?" he asked.

"It's an ointment for muscular aches and pains. You rub it in and it heats the area. The smell is soothing. It is intended to soothe the patient so that he relaxes and allows the muscle to relax. This helps the active ingredient to be absorbed into the inflamed tissue. The story is though that the 'vapour', as it is being called, causes hallucinations."

"What!"

"Yes. For the next few hours the patient is in cuckoo-land. Often he doesn't know who he is or where he is. He giggles and says inappropriate and silly things."

"Why is Mother Eleanor allowed to use it?"

"Because it is very successful with the muscle cramps. Afterwards the patient is most grateful. The pain is gone and he can live normally. As you can see a person who has been having muscular cramps will be delighted. Never mind the period of silliness which the patient claims to have enjoyed. But Mother Fulati says the hallucinations are a symptom of nerve poisoning. It may not be severe, and the patient may be back to normal in a few hours, but repeated use of it will almost certainly cause real harm. Even the patient's attendant is said to start giggling and behaving foolishly. Or did. I believe attendants are no longer allowed.

Mother Fulati is quite worried. So what she needs is for you to go and investigate. What ingredients is Eleanor using? If possible it would be wonderful if you could bring back a sample. Mother Fulati herself will decide what is to be done. I rely on her entirely in all such matters. She is our Wise Woman. It isn't surprising Eleanor likes to be called a witch! She doesn't sound wise."

"Yes of course I'll go," said Sonny. "And Gogo will come with me as usual?"

"Ceratainly. Start as soon as you can. I'll send a message of goodwill to the King of Beldeena, along with a request I have to think up. Once you are there look up Eleanor on Mother Fulati's behalf, and I'll have to leave the rest to you. You and Gogo need to talk to Mother Fulati first, and find out all you can from her. She might be able to suggest a line of approach. She will send you on one of her owls because they know the way, but take Goggles too. He could be very useful."

Gogo was quite excited about the long trip into mysterious territory as far as the Pongos were concerned. But first they went on Goggles' back to visit Mother Fulati. It was always a pleasure drawing in over the trees to land in her garden. Immediately they smelt the wonderful aroma of her plants. There were hundreds of varieties, each with a special property.

Both Mother Fulati and her daughter Selina were learned women. They had their own library full of books, but much, or most, of what they knew had been learnt from their mothers. The daughters of their line automatically started to learn to grow herbs and flowers as soon as they could walk, and along with growing them they learnt about their ingredients, and how they should be prepared and used in healing. Mother Fulati hurried out of her house drying her hands on her apron. Unlike the other Pongo women she always wore a long skirt with a short blouse fitted to the waist. When the weather was cool she wore a woolen shawl. She was not Pongo by ancestry, and her origins were unknown, though the word "Merlin" crossed Sonny's mind for the first time. Her family inter-married with others of their dynasty scattered across the Islands, though few were gifted with healing powers. Mother Fulati opened her arms to hug them both.

"Come along in! Selina has just made some scones, and they are hot from the oven. You would like a glass each of lime-juice wouldn't you?" They certainly would. Selina was a dark-haired light brown-skinned girl. She was wearing a full red skirt with a pink design on it and a pink blouse. They all sat down round the kitchen table while Mother Fulati told them about her worry regarding Eleanor's recent activities.

"I can't understand the woman! She knows it goes against all the rules to allow hallucigens to escape into the atmosphere. Very rarely a hallucigen might be prepared for purposes of allaying excess anxiety, or irrational fear, but the dose would always be tiny and never result in giggling and buffoonery. What she is doing has to be dangerous. And not only that, she is bringing disrepute to our profession. We have authority and respect because we understand our work. Who will trust us if we play about with peoples' minds?"

"How would you like us to approach this?" asked Sonny.

"You will meet the King first. Our King is giving us cover by writing to him to ask him for something. So when you have dealt with that you can show interest in the Island, but you can't waste a lot of time on a guided tour. Get to the point as quickly as you can. You can easily mention me because Eleanor is distantly related in our ancestry. Usually the gift of healing goes down through the direct line, but occasionally it will appear in a girl of another related line. Don't let on I sent you. Keep it general. Get yourselves to her house and after that you will have to play it by ear. What you want to know is the nature of some ointment she has for muscular aches and pains. Some new stuff. But since whatever it is seems to have become famous you can't ask outright, or she'll know why you've come. What you want is a sample to bring me and I will give you a little pot to put some in. Close it tightly to keep the aroma in. I can't say how you'll manage that," she said doubtfully.

"Steal it," said Gogo.

"No.......we aren't stealing it exactly. I don't want her ointment for my own work. I just need to check it out. A very small sample will be enough for me to test it for known hallucigens. If it is unknown to me that will mean there is something, possibly dangerous, growing on

Beldeena Isand which doesn't grow here. I outrank her in this work so I need to know what goes on."

She gave Gogo a little green pot, and after they had finished their refreshments she took them out into the garden.

"And while you are about it," she muttered, "get a look at Eleanor's son. I hear he is handsome and a good worker." Sonny looked startled.

"Her son? Does he live with her?"

"I think so, but whatever you do make sure you meet him. I want a good match for Selina."

"Oh!" said Sonny.

"Yes! Come on you two. You must know there is gossip on the Island about whom she will marry. He has to be of our lineage, but of course he won't be doing medical work. Could you find out what he does do? And I want to know what you think of him."

"Right," said Gogo.

As they flew off Gogo said the Sonny,

"Which do you believe is our primary task here?" Sonny grinned.

"Well practically speaking I think we need to take both tasks equally seriously if we are not to get a scolding! I did want to ask if her line goes back to Merlin, but with that Merido task being so confidential I daren't mention the subject. In a flash she would have been asking where we heard that!"

The journey to Beldeena involved two overnight stops so it wasn't until the third day that they arrived. As they approached they could see a river and rolling green hills. Sonny had learnt in his geography classes that just as the perimeters of the Islands dissolved into mist so that no-one could venture to the edge of an Island, so any rivers also vanished into the surrounding mist. Not only was visibility down to zero, but also the atmosphere resisted penetration. Nestling in a valley by the river was a town. Their attendant owl from Mother Fulati's home led Goggles to the town, and the two birds landed just outside in a grassy meadow.

The boys left them to rest and ventured into the town. Shops and houses lined both sides of the road, and narrower streets led off from it. Quite a few people were out shopping. They were of medium height and slender. They were brown-skinned of all shades from dark to very light brown. The women wore long wrap-around skirts with shirts, and the men wore trousers with similar shirts. Gogo approached a man coming up the road to ask him the way to the Palace. The man of course saw straight away that they were visitors, and they explained that they were from Pongoland. Sonny had realized few were likely to ask him why he looked different. Either people were too polite to mention it, or assumed some Pongo people looked like him.

"We don't often have visitors from Pongoland!" he exclaimed. "Welcome. You've come to see our King?"

"Yes, mainly, though we hope to see a little of Beldeena Island while we are here," said Gogo.

"Well I live along that road," the man pointed, "if you need any help. I am Petrie." The boys thanked him. "The Palace is near that roundabout you can see ahead. White marble."

They walked along to the roundabout and to their left saw high iron gates guarded by a sentry. The Palace was visible among trees behind. They could see the white pillars of a colonnade, and a high white dome. Sonny took the letter from their King out of his blue cotton satchel, and presented it to the sentry-man. The official lettering and the Pongoland crest on the envelope were sufficient for the gate to be opened to them. The boys were allowed in, and another official came out to meet them. He took them through the main door inside. Everything was built on a vast scale. There was a large hall with tiled floor, and a broad staircase to their left led up to the next floor. The dome above was paned so that the whole area was light and welcoming.

Sonny and Gogo were taken to a reception lobby and asked to sit for a moment. This room had large high windows and curtains which touched the floor. There was a big fire-place with mantel-piece, and the room was made inviting by several warm brightly-coloured rugs. Sonny and Gogo sat nervously.

Eventually a servant arrived and he invited them to go with him. They went along a corridor which led off the hall to a much larger sitting-room. Inside, there were the King and Queen, a boy about twelve and a younger girl. The Queen was reading aloud, but she stopped as they entered. It was approximately tea-time by then and there was a tray of refreshments on a low table in front of the fire-place. Sonny and Gogo were invited to join them. They were given a cup of tea and a slice of sponge-cake each. The King was holding the letter from the King of Pongoland in his hand.

"How are your King and Queen?" he asked. "It is several years since we visited your Island though we hope to be there this Summer for the Trade Fair. We have some very fine glass and crystal-ware to bring, as well as some of our famous rugs."

"Thankyou they are very well," said Sonny. "We look forward to seeing you at the Trade Fair."

"Let me see," said the King, putting on his glasses. "His majesty is interested in cross-breeding some of our sheep with yours? I don't know about that. There are all sorts of risks involved in cross-breeding."

Sonny and Gogo knew that the request was a ploy to introduce them on to the Island, and that he did not mind what the answer was. He could always "re-think" any idea later. How to get the subject of the conversation round to the Witch of Beldeena? Diplomacy was a really tough job, thought Sonny. The pitfalls were great and seemed to be scattered everywhere in the course of an apparently simple chat. Fortunately Gogo had sat through a good many in Pongoland, and knew how to ask a leading question in amongst politenesses about climate and scenery. Sonny was keen to learn a great deal in a very short time.

"We didn't notice any woodland as we came down," Gogo observed. "There is quite a lot in Pongoland."

"Yes, I remember," said the King. "You have that whole hill-side covered with trees, and Mother Fulati lives in the middle of them making medicines! We do have woodland, but it is over the other side. Everybody needs trees."

Sonny was about to ask a direct question but Gogo forestalled him by leading into the subject sideways.

"Of course," he said, "some Islands don't have enough and others have too many!"

"Well it is good that each Island has its' own special assets, and at the Trade Fair we can exchange our produce," said the Queen.

"Yes, things work pretty well," said Gogo." Mother Fulati takes samples of her remedies to the Fair and receives orders. Of course people from the Islands close to us just come over to see her if they need medical care."

"It is the same with our Madame Eleanor," said the King. "She makes medicines for us and heals people from neighbouring Islands."

"Is that so?" said Sonny. "And is she also old and wise?"

"I don't think either lady would like to be called old," laughed the Queen.

"Perhaps we might meet her while we are here, and see her work?" suggested Gogo.

"Of course, if you like," said the King. "Why not tomorrow after breakfast? How long do you expect to be here? I have to consult with our shepherds of course about the advisability of any cross-breeding."

"You will stay here of course," said the Queen, "and we'll arrange a pony-trap for you for tomorrow morning. It will be more interesting to see the Island from ground level, and I expect your owls will value a rest."

Things had gone pretty well the first evening, and Sonny and Gogo set off the next morning with high hopes. The King's son, Rick, accompanied them. This could be helpful or it could be awkward, but they had to take things as they unfolded. He was a cheerful boy and proved to be good company. He took the reins and pointed out the various sights. Each hill had a name. Some had sheep grazing on them and some did not. The hills where there were no sheep were partly built on. They could see flat-roofed houses with painted walls and little gardens. It was all very pleasant!

"Do people grow their own vegetables?" asked Sonny.

"Yes they do, quite a lot. The soil is very good, so it would be a waste not to," said Rick.

"I like it here," said Gogo, relaxing back and enjoying himself.

"Yes, we are a happy Island," said Rick. "Everyone helps each other and we have lots of parties and activities together. Of course my father is a good King and a lot depends on that."

"Who does Madame Eleanor live with?" asked Sonny. "Or does she live alone?"

"No she has a grown-up son, Gerard," said Rick. "His father is away quite a lot, but when he is at home he is of course also there."

"What does Gerard do?" asked Gogo.

"He is an artist and sculptor," said Rick.

"Wow!" said Sonny.

"Yes, he's very good. He does art work for the Island to barter, but people commission him to do portraits or whatever they want. He is also very good at room-designing. Décor. So people hire him for that. And he does sculptures for public places. Those of course are commissioned. He gets orders from other Islands."

"A talented family!" commented Gogo. "What does his father do?"

"He is a business-man for both Madame Eleanor and Gerard. He delivers and takes orders, and he advertises."

"Oh?" said Gogo, puzzled. Pongoland didn't have anyone like that because the King handled all exchanges with other Islands. Sonny too was doubtful about this role. The people of Pongoland never had to concern themselves about deliveries and orders.

"Our King does all of that," he felt forced to comment.

"I know," said Rick. "My father isn't happy about it. The Islands are small, and the King makes sure enough is produced of whatever is needed, and not too much of any item. And he monitors how much of what is imported from other Islands. Suddenly we've got Madrico wanting to barter some of his family's products himself with people on other Islands! My father hasn't said anything yet. He's waiting to see what happens. He feels there will be some crisis eventually which will make Madrico decide it would be better for the King to handle things. He's got a bit big for his boots since his son has proved so successful. Maybe he is jealous, I don't know, and wants to be important."

"What did he do before?" asked Gogo.

"He was also an artist, but not a very good one," said Rick. "Gerard is much more popular, and gets all the orders, so basically Madrico is put out!"

"Oh dear," said Sonny.

"Right," said Rick, "so it's a difficult situation, a delicate situation. That's why my father is letting him do his thing for a bit, and see how it pans out."

"And I suppose Madame Eleanor is also very much in demand," said Sonny.

"She certainly is. You don't get many people who understand plants well enough to be able to make medicines, so she is pretty famous too."

"And Dad is squashed between two unusually successful people," said Sonny.

"Yes, that's the situation," said Rick.

"Does he help Madame Eleanor at all in the preparation of the medicines?" asked Sonny. "Our Mother Fulati has a daughter, Selina, who works alongside her. It's a lot for one person to handle alone."

"He dabbles a bit I think," said Rick. "Well he does a lot of the heavy work in the garden, and he helps in gathering leaves or roots or seeds. He knows the plants, and all that would certainly be too much for Madame Eleanor to manage alone. He isn't a lazy man."

"But being a gardener isn't enough for him?" asked Gogo.

"No. He still does paintings, but demand for his work is poor."

By the time they reached Madame Eleanor's house Sonny and Gogo felt they had a good grasp of the general situation there. Madame Eleanor came to the door immediately. She was very surprised to see Prince Rick with two other boys about to knock. She had a low, stone-built house with a red-tiled roof, and like Mother Fulati she had a very large garden. Like Mother Fulati she wore an ankle-length full skirt with a short blouse. Her hair was long and grey and tied into a knot at the nape of her neck.

She smiled a welcome, and Prince Rick introduced Sonny and Gogo. They all went into the house straight into a big kitchen which was warm from an open fire. Things were brewing on an iron stove, and there were interesting aromas. A wooden table was scrubbed clean, and on it was a chocolate cake she had just baked. It was all so reminiscent of Mother Fulati's kitchen. They were invited to sit to the table and she cut three fat slices of cake for the boys. Rick told her they had come from Pongoland and were friends of Mother Fulati.

"She sends you greetings Ma'am," said Gogo, "and hopes you are all well."

"Thankyou," said Madame Eleanor. "Please tell her we are all well. I trust all is well with her. I hear Selina is a great help in her work."

"She is Madame, and is an expert now herself in making medicines," said Sonny.

"She was a promising child I remember," said Eleanor. "We all meet so rarely. We are busy women and haven't leisure to travel so far. What brings you here?"

Gogo said, "Our King wanted us to deliver a letter to your King."

"Well that's very nice," said Eleanor. "My son, Gerard, is out just now, but I expect him back any moment. I hope you can wait?"

"Yes we would love to meet him," said Gogo, looking at Sonny. "Might we look round your garden while we wait? Mother Fulati will be full of all sorts of questions when we get home."

Madame Eleanor was delighted at their interest and took them outside. Some plants were arranged in neat rows, others in square or rectangular patches. Trees lined the pathways, and Sonny could see fruits, and berries, and nuts.

"This is amazing," he said, "and I believe your woods are not far off?"

"No. I have been allotted part of the woods as an extension to my garden, so I have plenty of land for my needs."

"Do you experiment with new preparations as well as producing the regular recipes?" asked Sonny.

"I can see you have spent a lot of time with Mother Fulati! Like her I have many old books and manuscripts. We believe we are related way back somewhere. We have many preparations in common, and we have inherited the same style of dress. I imagine she experiments just as I do. You can't help it. You always try to extend your knowledge. You feel something might work better if you do this, or wonder, suppose I try that? It is always exciting and rewarding work."

"If you prepare a new remedy how do you test it?" asked Sonny.

"I apply it to myself first. I take larger doses than I would give patients, several times. That will show me if there are any unpleasant side-effects. When I am sure it is safe I give it to an appropriate patient, that is someone with the ailment I wish to treat. I warn the first few patients that this is something new, but they never mind because they know I have imbibed generous doses of it already myself. When it works I make careful notes with dates of every new preparation."

"Some of Mother Fulati's remedies have slight mind-altering effects," said Sonny. "They aren't harmful but are used to alleviate anxiety occasionally."

"Yes I too prescribe certain types of sedatives," said Eleanor, looking at Sonny.

"And do you make fruit juices or other things simply to eat or drink?" asked Sonny to change the subject.

"Yes certainly, and I prepare health drinks. Children love them. So do parents. Whenever I visit anybody's house I take along a bottle of one of my health drinks. That helps to maintain a good level of general health on the Island. Here is Gerard now!"

They saw a young man striding up the path. He was tall, brown skinned, dark haired, and handsome! Sonny and Gogo exchanged glances and small grins. He knew Rick of course, and his mother explained who Sonny and Gogo were.

"Let's go inside again," said Eleanor happily, "and I'll give you each a glass of fruit juice right now."

This was all very nice, thought Sonny, but how on earth to get round to the topic of the dodgy medicine? Desperate measures for desperate situations? As they sat down he asked conversationally,

"Mother Fulati heard you have a new ointment for rheumatism. She wondered what the ingredients are." Gogo stared at him hard.

"Rheumatism? Er......"

"You know the one Mum," said Gerard. "You used it on my arm when I sprained it, and it made me laugh."

"You mean it tickled?" asked Gogo interestedly.

"No. I just rolled around laughing," said Gerard, smiling at the memory.

"Goodness!" said Sonny. "What was in it to do that?"

"Gerard is exaggerating," said Eleanor hurriedly. "He was just being silly."

"No I wasn't Mum," he said. "I got a fit of the giggles and you gave me a big drink of water."

Madame Eleanor busied herself at the stove.

"You are exaggerating Gerard," she repeated.

"That could be useful if you need cheering up," said Rick helpfully. "Why don't you put a bit on my arm Ma'am and we'll see if I start laughing!"

Madame Eleanor turned round scarlet with anger.

"Please be quiet, all of you! You have no idea what you are talking about! You are all children, and you don't understand."

"Mum?" said Gerard, surprised.

"It was something I made at the request of your father. A client he had found in Ringoland wanted something to help his daughter. She had had a nasty fall from a tree and couldn't walk. She was very upset and frightened, and he wanted me to send something to help to make her cheerful again. Normally I wouldn't use that ingredient, but your father was desperate because this client had offered him a big commission to do the stage scenery for a play they were putting on in Ringoland. It was all that he could offer in exchange, and it meant so much to your father. I risked making up an ointment with the sap of a certain root added to it. The ointment was to work on her injured back and legs, and the sap was to lift her mood. But I hadn't calculated how much her father was going to apply. He seems to have ladled it on! She ended up in hysterics from an overdose of the sap, and it took a long time to quieten her. Her father was puzzled and very angry. I would have been in serious trouble except that when she woke up from a long sleep she was back to normal again and could walk! To her parents this was a miracle. The thick application of the ointment had seeped into the nerves and muscles of her back and revived them. There had been a miscalculation on my part. There should have been no sap, and a great deal more of the ointment applied than I had prescribed."

86

Sonny and Gogo listened fascinated. They were all thrilled to hear about the outcome, but realized that in adult work there are risks and chances of things going badly wrong. It is not always happy-ever-after. Madame Eleanor had understood her husband's frustration when his son turned out to be much more successful than he was, even though at the same time he was very proud of his son. So she had acted against her better judgment, hoping to win him the commission. He did get it, but she had been very lucky not have had her reputation ruined.

Sonny thought about this.

"Sometimes you take risks," he said. "You have to sometimes."

"Yes Sonny," said Madame Eleanor. "That is so true. The problem is that if you don't take a risk sometimes you can't learn. That little girl was very seriously injured. I had just needed to know in such a case at least double the normal dose is necessary."

"I have the same sort of fears in my work too," said Gerard. "When I am asked to carve a statue they give me a huge slab of marble or some other stone, and I have to hack away at it, and chip at it, often just hoping for the best. It could end up ludicrous. I have to see the final result in my mind's eye, and then as an image in the stone, and chip away until it emerges for everyone else to see, but that too can be very scary."

Sonny and Gogo felt very sober listening to them revealing the anxieties they experienced in the course of a normal day's work.

"You are very brave," said Sonny. "The Islands are very lucky to have people like you."

Eleanor bent over and kissed him.

"And you have a wise head on young shoulders," she said.

"May we have a look at it? The ointment?" Gogo asked. Eleanor lifted down a large jar from a shelf and took off the lid.

"This is the stuff," she said. They looked at it and sniffed.

"It has a strange smell," said Sonny.

"Yes. Quite a few ingredients go into it, and they don't all smell nice. This has no sap in it. Never again!"

"Can I tell Mother Fulati about this?" asked Sonny. "She would be very interested, and I am sure she would understand about the sap."

"Yes. Tell her. But these things are NOT to be told to other people. Do you understand?"

"Yes Ma'am," said Sonny and Gogo respectfully. "But I wonder, might I tell our King also?"

"Yes. Kings need to know these things. He wouldn't dream of talking about it," she said. "It is such a long time since I met Mother Fulati I do believe we should pay her a visit. Would you tell her we will come to Pongoland in a little while, the three of us? We can't write to each other easily, but tell her April!"

"She will be thrilled!" said Gogo.

"Tell her I will bring her a pot of my ointment," said Madame Eleanor.

"Madame Eleanor," said Sonny, "we heard people call you the Witch of Beldeena. Do you mind being called a witch?"

"Yes I am referred to sometimes as 'the witch'," said Eleanor. "It is meant affectionately by the people of this Island, as much as anything because to say 'Madame Eleanor' is a mouthful! But it isn't incorrect. A white witch works with Nature to perform her healing. She studies to understand Nature, and treats Nature with respect and reverence. In that sense I am a witch. For the white witch the law is 'do no harm'. Any magic I use is the magic hidden within Nature itself. I just harness what is there already for a healing purpose."

"I see yes, thankyou," said Sonny.

The boys returned to the Palace in the late afternoon after a ride around the Island. Sonny and Gogo felt deeply content with their visit to Beldeena, and with their visit to Madame Eleanor.

That evening the King told them that the shepherds did not favour the idea of cross-breeding any of their sheep with Pongoland sheep.

"They say the risk of compromising the purity of both breeds is too great, and this would result in a degradation in the quality of their wool," he said.

"That's fine Sir," said Gogo. "We'll take the message back. I hope we will meet you at the Trade Fair."

"Sir," said Sonny tentatively, "we learnt a strange thing today. You know all about it already so we can speak of it. We heard Madame

Eleanor's husband is engaged in bartering some of her remedies with people on other Islands, and even taking orders for art-work to be done by Gerard from other Islands. That is very unusual surely?" The King sighed.

"Yes. We are having a problem there. Of course Eleanor's work has always been negociated by me. In return for her services abroad we get vetinary services, for instance, in return. Other things too from different Islands. In return for Gerard's public art works abroad we get construction work done in Beldeena. The negociations there are specific, piece by piece, and I look after it. There are other art exchanges also on a piece by piece basis, individually arranged. All done by me. Then suddenly Madrico starts swapping his wife's remedies for "favours" really. He was distressed because orders for his own art work dropped off as Gerard's work became so popular. So he started trying to promote his own work abroad. He would persuade people to allow him to do a painting where it would be generally visible in return for some general remedies from his wife's cupboard. She, poor lady, didn't want to hurt his feelings even more. He acted on Gerard's behalf too. A portrait done by Gerard if a second portrait was ordered to be done by himself. What could Gerard say? I was waiting a while because I knew what he was doing wouldn't work in the long run. It runs counter to the entire economy of the Islands. In the end he would be sure to realize that himself. It looks as if that moment has come. I will sort it out. I'll try and give him work to do himself. He works very hard in their garden but obviously he needs artistic outlet."

"That's alright then," said Sonny. "I do hope he's soon back on track. We should leave in the morning Sir. We have had a wonderful visit here. Thankyou very much for everything."

The next morning Goggles arrived with Mother Fulati's owl outside the Palace to pick them up. After many goodbyes, and messages of good will to the Royal Family of Pongoland, they finally set off. The King had given them an interesting-looking parcel to deliver to their King and Queen.

The King was over-joyed to hear they were safely home and in good spirits. The boys went first to the Palace to make their report. They told the King and Queen the full story of the ointment laced with a mysterious sap, and the happy outcome. They listened intently, understanding full well the risk Eleanor had taken for her husband. They were very experienced themselves in the snags and pitfalls which lay in the path of all those in places of responsibility. They were the last to judge anyone who tripped on one. They too understood how much was learnt by experience, and sometimes bitter experience. You earned wisdom. It didn't come free. They appreciated also the dilemma faced by the King in handling such a sensitive issue. Such problems were not unusual in the life of a King. The parcel turned out to be a fine painting done by Gerard of a unicorn standing by a forest pool in moonlight. It was breath-takingly beautiful, and the King and Queen gasped with pleasure.

After leaving the Palace they asked Goggles to take them to Mother Fulati's house. Her own owl had gone straight back home so she would know they were coming. She too listened with great interest to the story of the ointment. She was impressed with the cure it had brought about in so severe an injury, and thrilled to be given a jar of it for herself to look at. She said that healing is learnt equally through inherited knowledge, from books, and by experience. Then she took them into the garden to ask,

"And what about her son? What's he like?"

"Amazing! Tall, handsome, and already a renowned artist in their part of the world! Madame Eleanor hints that they will come to Pongoland in April!" said Gogo.

"Ah," said Mother Fulati.

"But where would they live?" asked Sonny. "Gerard is doing so well there. He isn't likely to want to move here. And how would you manage if Selina left you?"

"I would employ somebody good with plants," said Mother Fulati. "We can't arrange other peoples' lives for them. In the future they might choose to make this place their home. Who knows? Things change and you have to let them. After all my own family didn't always live in Pongoland. It is said our remote ancestors lived in Meridoland."

Back in Gogo's house, after registering Mother Fulati's bomb-shell, Sonny and Gogo were happy to relax. The Murgos were just thankful to have them back safe and sound. The long trips, unescorted, had been frightening for them, however much they trusted the owls. No-one had ever forgotten Anton's disappearance. No bird even had ever brought any news. Now, with the three tests successfully completed they too were in a mood to celebrate.

"Goggles needs a day's rest tomorrow," said Murgo, "so you can take Sonny home on Wobbles, Gogo." Wobbles was a deputy to Goggles, to be called on occasionally when needed.

"Now, come along all of you," said Mrs Murgo. "A feast is ready for all you heroes."

Murgo stood up and shook both the boys' hands.

"Well done both of you," he said. "Very well done."

Gogo and Sonny were too embarrassed to speak, but Sonny felt he would remember Murgo's words for the rest of his life, and hoped that for the rest of his life he would be worthy of them.

About the Author

Jennifer Hashmi was born in Bradford and attended Bingley Grammar School. She trained as a speech therapist in Leicester, and did a theology course in College of Ascension Birmingham. In 1964 she sailed for India and lived there forty years. In 1977 she married Salman Hashmi and has a son and a daughter. In 2005, after her husband's passing, she returned to England, and lives with her daughter, son-in-law, and grandson. She wrote "Sonny, Gogo, Tobo, and their adventures", and "Merriol and the Lord Hycarbox " in India. "Further Adventures of Sonny, Gogo, and Tobo" was written in England.

Lightning Source UK Ltd.
Milton Keynes UK
UKOW02f0012050516

273568UK00001B/8/P